"Why are you still putting it on the line like this?" George asked

Dan Track looked at his nephew and shrugged. "Sometimes," he began, "somebody has to say, 'Hey—this crap can't go on.' But it's going to keep going on unless I try to stop it."

He looked away from George and stared out the window. "Working for the Consortium gives me the opportunity to do stuff that no cop can do. I can play by whatever rules I want. I can use the same rules the bad guys use and nail their asses to the wall."

Track turned back into the room. "You understand what I mean?"

TRACK
The Hard Way

JERRY AHERN

A GOLD EAGLE BOOK FROM
WORLDWIDE

TORONTO · NEW YORK · LONDON · PARIS
AMSTERDAM · STOCKHOLM · HAMBURG
ATHENS · MILAN · TOKYO · SYDNEY

For William J. Devine, faithful reader and correspondent—all the best, my friend....

Special thanks to Sid Woodcock for technical assistance—it's a good thing for everyone that he's on our side.

———————————◆—◆———————————

First edition December 1984

ISBN 0-373-62004-7

Printed in Canada

1

Dan Track clenched the SPAS-12 in both fists and crawled ahead silently and slowly on his knees and elbows, listening. But all he could hear were the sounds of his own movement and stray noises coming from the dozen men behind him, a well-trained strike force. To his right his nephew, George Beegh, was gripping an Aimpoint-sighted M-16 as he made his way through the high grass. Looking to his left, Track saw his old friend Lew Wilson, a senior agent with the Florida Department of Law Enforcement, moving through the field, cradling another M-16.

Through the earphone in his left ear, Track heard the insectlike buzz of his radio. He snapped his fingers once in George's direction, and George glanced at him briefly, nodding, then used hand and arm signals to slow the men to his right. Track snapped his fingers to his left, but Lew Wilson had heard the prearranged signal and was already motioning the left flank of the strike force to a halt.

Dan Track rolled onto his back. The Florida sunlight was warm and strong on his face. He squinted against it and set the SPAS-12 in the grass beside him, then removed the small radio set from his belt and depressed the talk button with his left thumb. "This is Track. Go ahead, Sir Abner. Over," he whispered.

Sir Abner Chesterton's voice crackled through the earphone. "Dan, the ransom pickup has been made by two men, both likely Israelis. We've managed to get a make on only one of them. Carlo Capezi's men are being held back—Capezi has ordered them to wait until you signal that you have the girl. Over."

Track growled into the headset. "You make certain they stay on the other side of the highway where the Don said they would. Last thing we need is a bunch of syndicate soldiers smashing their way in here—they don't hire enforcers because of their woodsmanship. Over."

"Roger on that, Dan," Sir Abner's British voice came back. "The radioactive isotope we put on the ransom money has apparently worked. The Israelis switched the money to a different satchel, leaving behind our bag with the low-frequency homing device, but the radiological people have a reading on the isotope. As Agent Wilson predicted, the pickup men are heading into your area. Over."

Track nodded to the radio set automatically, as if somehow Sir Abner could see him, then searched the inside breast pocket of his bomber jacket with his free hand and found his black leather cigar case. Using thumb and forefinger, he opened the case as he talked. "What's their ETA here? Over."

There was a long pause, punctuated by some background noise filtering through the earphone. Track guillotined one of the Cuesta-Rey Six-Ts, stuck it in the left corner of his mouth and bit down on it. Sir Abner's voice came back. "Dan—we estimate they should cross the contact point at the highway junction in five—repeat, five—minutes. Over."

Track loosened his hold on the cigar. "Once they cross the junction," he whispered into the radio, "have the radiological team pull back. There's rough country this side of the road, and I don't want the two Israelis to get slowed down and the radiological team to bump into them. Keep me posted. Track out."

He replaced the radio handset in the leather carrier on his belt. Wilson and George were both watching him.

Track held up his right hand, his fingers and thumb splayed to indicate five minutes.

Wilson nodded. George pulled his Jack Daniels baseball cap low over his forehead. Both men passed the signal to the men of the strike force behind them.

Track rolled onto his belly, taking up the SPAS-12 again, and crawled ahead. Half the open field had already been crossed, but it was another twenty-five yards to the tree line. Behind him, the strike force spread out on both sides for an eighth of a mile.

Track kept moving. Shooting the cuff of his bomber jacket, he glanced at the watch and did some quick mental calculations. Eighteen minutes to 2:00 P.M. At thirteen minutes to two, the Israeli pickup team should be crossing the road on foot, moving into the trees behind the strike force, then traversing the open field on their way to the swamp beyond the trees. Wilson had employed aerial-reconnaissance and ground maps to suggest that the Israelis were using an abandoned research station in the swamp as their base, as the place they kept Don Carlo Capezi's twenty-three-year-old daughter hostage. With the current direction of the two bagmen, it looked as if Wilson had been right. Track moved ahead as rapidly as he could, hugging the profile of the ground, tiring from the fifty-yard-crawl across the clear field.

The rogue Israeli commandos who had abducted the girl had made the usual threat—at one hint of the authorities, she would be killed instantly. But with these men there were no threats, only promises. And Dan Track had no doubt the Israelis would keep the promise. They had done so in the kidnapping of computer designer Franz Heigler. Heigler had been heavily insured by one of the member companies of the Consortium, and the insurer had decided to hold back, against Track's and Sir Abner's wishes. The ransom eventually had been paid, but Franz Heigler had been found in a ditch on a dirt road near the edge of a swamp, his throat slit, his body floating on the surface of the green slimy water, putrefaction producing enough gas to bloat the body and cause it to rise. Heigler had been identified only by his dental records. The Israelis had murdered him, and one of the Consortium subscribers was out five million dollars.

Don Carlo Capezi's daughter was also insured by one of the Consortium member companies, but the total payoff value of her policy was less than thirty-five thousand dollars. Track, George Beegh and Sir Abner Chesterton weren't defending just the financial interests of the Consortium this time—the operation had so far cost the Consortium twice the value of the policy covering the young woman.

They were moving through the clearing now, toward the trees toward the swamp beyond for one reason only: legal revenge. After the affair with Johannes Krieger and the stolen five-hundred-kiloton thermonuclear warheads, Track had set out ground rules for his and George's continued work with the Cartel of International Insurance Underwriters known as the Consortium. If his and George's job was to be the foiling of international terrorists and major criminals, revenge— within the context of the law when possible, outside the confines of law when necessary—was vitally important.

To have any effect at all beyond what conventional authority could do, Track had realized, the commission of a terrorist act or a major crime that in any way affected or held the potential to affect persons or property insured by Consortium member companies had to carry with it the automatic knowledge that when law enforcement, the military and all others had given up, Dan Track would not. There would be retribution—the Cartel of International Insurance Underwriters had agreed to this.

As he moved into the tree line, rising up into a

crouch, sweeping the area immediately in front of him under the muzzle of the SPAS-12, Track reflected that this was most definitely an operation falling under the heading of retribution.

Over the past several years in the United States a new Mafia had been emerging, but none of the members was Sicilian. Some of them were former Israeli military and intelligence personnel who had left their homeland or, in some cases, left their adopted homeland and returned to the land of their birth. All of them were highly trained and highly lethal. All of them gave new depth of meaning to the term "cold-blooded."

When the Black Hand, the original name of the Sicilian Mafia, had begun its assault on the United States a century earlier, infiltration had been doubly difficult for law-enforcement personnel because of the language barrier, the strong cultural ties and the family nature of the criminal society. The new syndicate, known as the Malina, presented all these obstacles and more. The Malina displayed a sophisticated tactical intelligence and put unbearable pressure on ordinary police forces. Specially trained antiterrorist units were also severely tested wherever the Malina operated.

Track covered George as the younger man reached the tree line and George's M-16 in turn provided cover for Lew Wilson as he gained the shelter of the trees after George. Track retrieved the radio from his belt and glanced at his watch as he depressed the talk button— the five minutes had passed. "Track to Sir Abner. Over."

There was a moment's pause before Sir Abner's voice crackled through the earphone. "Chesterton here, Dan. I was just about to signal you. The two Israelis have crossed the highway junction on foot and should be entering the trees opposite you on the road side of the clearing in—let me double-check that, stand by—"

Track watched as the law-enforcement strike force

fanned into the tree line. Then Sir Abner's voice was back.

"Make that two minutes at their present pace. We have visual confirmation of that from the rise a half mile south of your position. Over."

"Contact me as soon as they hit the opposite treeline. Let me know if they change direction or do anything funny. Track out." Track replaced the radio set on his belt and, using hand and arm signals, communicated the whereabouts of the Israelis and their ETA at the tree line on the opposite side of the clearing.

As he finished, he could hear the hiss of whispers and the stray rattles of loose sling swivels as the men of the strike force—Justice Department and state and local SWAT teams—took to the trees.

Track slung the SPAS-12, its own sling swivels taped for silence, cross-body, muzzle down, over his back. Then he sized up the oak tree beside him and decided that it seemed adequate. "George—give me a leg up," he said softly.

His nephew nodded and clasped his fingers together behind his back. Track placed his left foot in George's hands and boosted himself against the tree, reaching for the lowest limb above him. Then he swung his right leg up into the crook of the branch, easing back into the leafy cover.

Fortunately the tree wasn't crawling with ants, Track thought, as he watched Wilson, unaided, scale a smaller tree about ten yards away. Below, Track watched as George took back several steps backward, then came at the oak tree in a run. He jumped, his hands clawing at the limb to Track's left, his legs swinging up.

George eased back into the notch and leaned against the trunk, less than eight inches from Track's left shoulder. He reached under his Levi's jacket and produced the paperback novel Track had given him and which he had been reading for the past two days in bits and snatches—

one of the ubiquitous novels in the adventure series called The Takers, the author a man named Josh Culhane.

Track looked at his nephew and arched his eyebrows. "Ah, George," he began. "Don't you think you're being a bit too nonchalant?"

George appeared not to hear. "You know," he whispered, holding up the thick paperback, "I don't understand what the hell you see in this stuff. Bang, bang, shoot 'em up—too much like our lives lately. This Sean Dodge character should have got shot ten times in the first chapter!"

"You could say the same thing about us," Track replied. "But this isn't a book. Which reminds me, you'd better—"

Track was interrupted by the buzzing of the radio in his ear, followed by Sir Abner Chesterton's voice. "Dan—they've entered the trees by the road. Broke into a run when they did. They're coming your way fast. Chesterton out."

Track snapped his fingers once, then once again, hearing single snaps from various spots among the trees as the squad leaders for the strike force answered. They were ready.

Track tapped George on the shoulder, and George put the adventure novel away, nodding.

At the far edge of the clearing, Track could see the two Israelis as they broke from the trees. One of them was carrying a stuff sack under his right arm.

The ransom money—one million dollars in cash— would be inside, irradiated with a short-half-life, highly radioactive isotope.

The men ran openly through the high grass of the field, crossing it in little more than a minute. Track would be watching them slow up as they reached the cover of the trees in which he and the others were hidden. In his right fist, he held the Metalife Custom L-Frame Smith & Wesson .357.

Both the Israelis were tall thin men. One had dark features, the other fair, with a bushy mustache. They paused at the edge of the trees as if studying their surroundings.

The blond guy was looking up into the trees, a pistol in his hand. Track edged his right index finger against the trigger of the L-Frame, ready.

The dark-haired Israeli said something Track couldn't understand, but Track recognized it as Russian, not the Hebrew he'd expected to hear. The blond answered in a rough whisper, then both men started through the tree cover, the fair-haired one passing directly under the oak in which Track and George were hidden.

Track watched as the two Israelis disappeared in the direction of the swamp and the research station. Beside him, George was removing the radiation-detection monitor from the GI map-and-photo case that he was carrying. There was an audible click as George activated the switch. He grinned and gave a thumbs-up signal.

Track turned to his right. Lew Wilson was already starting down out of the tree.

Track reached out along the limb, getting a handhold, then swung into midair and let go, dropping soundlessly to the ground.

George tossed down the radiation monitor to his uncle, then jumped down, rolling slightly forward before coming up into a crouch.

Track had brought the SPAS-12 forward on its sling and held the riot shotgun ahead of him like a wand as he studied the meter on the radiation monitor. From the decreasing strength of the signal, he knew the Israelis were moving fast. He started into a long-strided commando walk through the tree cover and toward the swampy area beyond, with George and Lew Wilson flanking him.

If he lost the Israelis, the girl's life would be lost—once the ransom was paid, she'd be butchered. He held no illusions to the contrary.

Leaving the rest of the strike force behind as a fall-back force, Track, George Beegh and Lew Wilson took up the trail alone.

2

The Israelis had skirted the swamp, as Dan Track had guessed they would. Hiding in the bracken, Lew Wilson spoke to Track softly and rapidly. "From the aerial photos I showed you, the research station should be just around that inlet, past the sandbar and then beyond those trees."

"What was the station used for?" Track asked.

"Alligators are on the upswing as a species now," Wilson replied, "but several years ago they weren't. The research station was used for studying breeding habits, stuff like that. All the people involved did a good job, I guess—we're getting enough gators down here to trip over them now."

As if to punctuate his words, the water immediately before them rippled and there was a slapping, splashing sound. The surface broke and the snout of one of the reptiles appeared, its mouth opening in what looked like a yawn.

To his right, Track heard George muttering, "I don't like it here."

Track slapped his nephew's shoulder. "Relax, we're not crossing the swamp. We're going around it—"

Wilson interrupted him. "That's more dangerous, really. The gators like to slither in and out of the water sometimes. In a good boat you'd be reasonably safe."

"See—I told ya—I don't like it here," George insisted.

Track pushed himself up from his crouch, eyeing the

Israelis as they disappeared into the trees on the other side of the wetland. "Let's go," Track urged.

"I'm for that," George agreed.

As they moved, Track could hear Lew speaking into his radio. "This is Wilson. Strike force move up into position on the near side of the swamp, then follow us— map reference seventeen. Move out."

There was the sound of metal rubbing metal as Wilson lowered the radio antenna. Track glanced back at him. In Track's hands, its stock collapsed, was the SPAS-12, both safeties on, the 8-round tubular magazine loaded with 2-3/4 double 0 buck, the ninth round in the chamber the same.

Around him were the noises of birds, the splashing sounds of the gators and squishing sounds, as the mud that formed the boundary between the dry land and the swamp sucked at the soles of his combat boots. They kept down, moving beyond a low line of scrub brush that grew just beyond the brown mud border.

Track glanced at his watch as he broke into a crouched run. It had taken the Israeli commandos eighteen minutes to go around the swamp. He wanted to do it in nine.

He had watched the Israelis as they had moved around the ragged perimeter of the swamp, having George note on the aerial map the points where they had slowed their course or zigzagged. Occasionally he pulled up to confirm a visual reference point with the map.

"Here, there should be something here," he whispered.

"Dan—looks like punji sticks over here," Wilson called out, his voice low. Track crept forward. In the soft mud, spikes—not of bamboo but of steel—were positioned around a platform, forming a ragged, angular figure eight. Stepping on the metal platform would launch the spikes upward into the feet. Track reached into his hip pocket and extracted a Puma 970 lockblade folding hunting knife. One-handed, he flicked it open, using the tip of the English Bowie-pattern blade to stencil into the mud around the platform of spikes.

"Why don't you just release them?" George asked, kneeling in the mud beside him.

Track said nothing as he leaned across the platform of spikes, clearing away mud, exposing a portion of coaxial cable. "That's why. When the platform goes off it triggers an alarm, which in turn probably aims some sort of parabolic microphone or a camera at the spot to pick up whether it was a human or some animal that wandered into the trap by mistake."

Track edged back, looking ahead and upward. He had seen a glint of light before. The sun was dropping fast now, and he would have better luck eluding conventional cameras—like the object he was convinced was mounted in the tree twenty-five yards ahead—than infrared heat sensors or night-vision equipment. "Follow me," he said, not wasting time to say any more.

There were two more of the spike-inlaid platforms, pressure sensitive like the first, and near each of these a television camera was placed for visual monitoring. There was a significant disadvantage to electronic surveillance equipment in wild country with heavy animal and bird populations—it could trigger at the wrong times. But Track counted this his advantage. Men disturbed in the middle of poker games, meals, sleep periods and the like by a stray bobcat disrupting an electronic defense grid would after a time expect the "intruder" to be some hapless wild creature. This expectation would slow their response times, slow their reactions.

Already nine minutes had elapsed, two of these minutes consumed traversing a crosshatched field of sensor wires in a clearing two-thirds of the way around the perimeter of the swamp. Of necessity having to keep low to avoid random visual observation, they had crossed the field of wires like snakes making their way through a backyard that was prepared for a croquet match. And Wilson had left, as he had beside the three platforms of spikes, a trail sign warning the strike force personnel coming after them.

Twelve minutes into the pursuit around the swamp, Track signaled a halt. They had reached the clearing into which the two Israelis had disappeared. Wilson whispered, "The research station should be about two hundred yards in."

"That place should be wired like crazy—from here to there," George began. "It's going to take—"

Track interrupted him. "You run the hundred pretty fast, George?"

"Yeah, I run pretty fast." George nodded, his dark eyes looking puzzled as beads of perspiration tracked down his forehead.

"I can run pretty good, too," Wilson added. "You thinking what I think you're thinking?"

Track turned to Lew Wilson. "Only way in there as far as I can tell. We should be able to make it in less than forty-five seconds. George hits the right side. You hit the left. You said there was one front door and one back door. Well, I hit the front door. You guys go around the sides and storm your way in the back."

"You're the visiting fireman," Wilson said as he grinned. "Hell, you're not even a cop. *I* go in the front door. You and George take the back."

"Yeah, but I've got this," Track said, holding up the SPAS-12. "You said the station measures twenty-five by fifteen, single floor. Imagine what nine doses of double 0 buck will do in there. Once I get in, I'll pinpoint Capezi's daughter and keep everyone away from her—so you guys had better make it in fast. And just as you go around the side, Lew, call in your strike force to back us up." Track handed George his radio—the one linked to Sir Abner Chesterton at the command post—then pulled the plug from his ear and passed it to his nephew.

"George," Track muttered, "when you go around the side, call in Sir Abner's people. His choppers should be ready to get off the ground and be here in under three minutes."

"I don't know how many men are in there," Wilson said. "We may be awful busy for three minutes. It'll take my strike force at least that long to catch up with us."

Dan Track grinned. "Well, after these are gone," he said, tapping the magazine of the SPAS, "I've got plenty more," and he patted the outside patch pockets of his leather bomber jacket.

Lew Wilson smiled and worked off the safety on his M-16. "You ready?"

"I was born ready!" Track said. He saw the other two look at him and he shrugged and added, "I heard Ward Bond say it in a western." With George and Lew Wilson flanking him, Track pushed himself to his feet. He held the SPAS at high port and broke into a dead run for the gray-green, corrugated-metal research station.

For a moment there was nothing but the sound of their boots hitting the dust-dry ground between the sparsely planted pine trees. Then Track heard George shouting, "Dan! Trip wires—could be weapons rigged!"

Track glanced right. George, outdistancing him by about ten yards, was jumping a series of barely discernible wires. Track looked ahead, seeing them, jumping, jumping again. A burst of machine gunfire from behind startled him, and he heard Wilson shout, "Almost bought it that time!" Track glanced back in time to see Wilson pull himself out of a stumble, regain his balance, then run full tilt again.

From the front of the corrugated hut came three

bursts of assault-rifle fire. Track worked off the SPAS-12's safety, firing from the hip as he ran. He judged the distance to the hut to be less than forty yards, and the sounds of the .30-caliber pellets from the SPAS hammering at the corrugated metal of the building sounded like hail on a tin roof. Track fired again, and the window to the right of the door burst inward.

George and Lew Wilson were breaking off, running toward the sides of the building, their assault rifles blazing with even, 3-round bursts. Windows across the front of the building shattered in response, and the front door caved partially inward as Track fired three more rounds of the double 0 buck. From his left-front patch pocket, he was pulling fresh shells, ramming them into the magazine tube. He fired three fast rounds and hurtled himself against the door.

He crashed through, coming down hard in a roll across the floor of the hut as assault-rifle fire hammered through windows on both sides of the building. Men were moving around him, some of them half dressed. Pistols discharged into the floor near him as he rolled again, firing the SPAS twice, ripping a rifle-armed defender in two at the waist.

As the wall behind him was peppered with submachine gunfire, Track stabbed the SPAS outward and unleashed two more rounds into the crowd of surprised bodies, rolled behind the cover of a packing crate and went flat, ramming fresh rounds into the SPAS's magazine. The crate disintegrated in a storm of slivers as more submachine gunfire ripped into the boards.

Track sprinted away from the wall, working the trigger of the SPAS-12, cutting down every living thing he saw as his eyes searched for the Capezi girl.

Then he spotted her in the corner—and his stomach churned.

Track wheeled away from what he saw, feeding more rounds into the SPAS's tubular magazine.

Suddenly the back door of the hut burst open and Lew Wilson was framed in the doorway. "Police! You're all under arrest!" he shouted.

Track and Wilson opened fire simultaneously as the half-dozen-or-so Malina still alive in the hut charged toward the front door.

The window on the back wall of the hut smashed inward as a chunk of log the thickness of a telephone pole and about three feet long came flying through it.

Some of the Malina turned from the front door, firing toward it. George stood framed in the rear doorway, the M-16 in his right fist and the .45 Combat Government in his left both spitting fire in the hazy gray light of the hut.

Track emptied the SPAS and surveyed the scene. The place had the look of a crude slaughterhouse as chunks of flesh littered the hut, while blood congealed on the floor and stained the walls.

There was a shout from behind a stack of wooden crates in the far rear corner of the hut. "We surrender! We surrender!"

Dan Track wheeled toward the sound, fresh shells going into the magazine of the SPAS, the shotgun leveled at his hip.

It was Lew Wilson's voice that shouted, "We're the law, Dan—not assassins!"

Overhead, Track could hear the beating of chopper blades, the occasional crackle of machine-gun or assault-rifle fire and unintelligible commands being broadcast over bullhorns in the air above and on the ground outside the hut.

A few Israelis had got through the front door after he'd crashed inside—and he'd been happy to let them leave. They obviously hadn't made it far.

Track started toward the crates, the SPAS ready. The middle knuckles of his left hand were bleeding where he'd scraped them against the floor when he'd come through the doorway. His right ankle was sore, and he remembered twisting it a little when he'd ducked behind the packing crate. Other than that, he was all right.

"Throw out your guns. Come out with your hands on your heads," Track shouted toward the crates, now less than ten feet from him diagonally across the hut.

There was a moan and a thud, and Track hit the floor. To Track's left, Wilson shouted, "There's a small storage area beneath the hut. Maybe they've dug an escape tunnel out from there—"

Track fired three fast rounds from the SPAS, then leaped up and charged the packing crates, knocking over the top crate with a solid kick.

He stepped around the side of the crates, shoving the toppled ones away with his left foot. There was a trapdoor.

"George," Track shouted. "Get on to Sir Abner— have him alert the choppers to look for people coming out somewhere in the trees around the hut."

Track yanked the lid of the trapdoor up; assault-rifle fire tore through it as he fell back.

On the floor, edging away from the trapdoor, Track reloaded the SPAS-12.

"The girl—my God—" It was Wilson.

Track glanced back across the single room of the hut. He looked at Wilson—there was no need to look again at the girl. She had been dead for more than a day, he realized. Her body was discolored and lividity had already set in. The blanket covering her had been partially pulled away when Track shot one of the Israelis and his body had sprawled back across hers. Her throat had been slit and she was naked.

"Mother of God," Wilson shouted as he stood over the body of Angelina Capezi.

"All right—we kill these bastards my way," Track snarled. He could hear the crackle of the radio as George talked to Sir Abner.

"You can't, Dan," Wilson shouted.

Track held a half-filled gasoline can in his hands, taken from the supply he guessed was used to power the small generator he'd seen outside. "I'm going to burn the bastards out," Track shouted, but he winked at Wilson.

Men from the strike force were filling the building as Track stepped back from the trapdoor. He glanced at Wilson, at George and at the others. "Be ready. If there's a way out, we go in after them. If there isn't another way out, they'll come out this way—and fast."

Track opened the can of gasoline, popping the plastic vent-hole cover. He edged forward on his hands and knees toward the yawning trapdoor.

Assault-rifle fire streamed up from the space beneath the hole. Track shouted, "Lew, George—fill that hole with some fire of our own!"

For a moment the room reverberated with the staccato, high-pitched thudding of .223s and the sound of brass cartridge casings ricocheting off floors and walls.

Track edged forward, keeping low beneath the friendly fire until he was within reach of the hole. He pushed the can over, and the contents spilled out of the gooseneck and down into the storage area.

There were shouts, followed by a burst of subgun fire. Then, as Track rocked back on his heels and onto his back, swinging the SPAS up and on line, men drenched with the gasoline scrambled up into the hut.

Track had the carry safety off, and his right index finger twitched back against the trigger of the SPAS-12. The weapon roared and one of the commandos went down, followed by another and another as the SPAS repeated its message. Two more Malina terrorists were caught in a cross fire as Wilson's voice shouted again over the din, "Police! Drop your weapons and get your hands up!"

A wiry man Track recognized as one of the ransom

carriers stumbled up from the trapdoor, a submachine gun in his hands. Track fired the SPAS, and the man's head ripped away from his neck and torso. The body crashed back into the submachine-gun-armed man behind him.

Track's shotgun belched death again, delivering a center of mass hit to a man carrying an Uzi.

And then it stopped—no more men came through the trapdoor.

Track heard a shouted plea. "I surrender! There are two men down here with me who are hurt. We give up!"

Track looked at Wilson, shrugging. Lew Wilson only nodded, saying, "Yeah, rules are made for kids and cops. Everybody else breaks them." Then Wilson shouted toward the opening, "One man will slowly throw out each weapon down there. At the first sight of a gun as you leave the cellar, we will open fire. Start throwing out the weapons now!"

Track edged back.

In the corner of the room, his eyes found the girl again, found her eyes, dead, glazed and staring. In some cultures, he recalled, there was a belief that the eye retained the image last seen at the moment of death. If it was true, Dan Track thought as he reloaded the SPAS, Angelina Capezi saw a butcher. And the horrible vision would be in her eye until her eye turned to dust.

3

Dan Track sat on a tree stump, smoking one of his Cuesta-Rey Six-Ts and watching the scene at the research station ten yards or so away from him. If someone had asked him if anything would ever have made him feel sorry for a convicted mobster and underworld boss, one of the highest-ranking mafiosi in the United States, his answer would have been, "No."

He inhaled the smoke from his cigar and blew it out. He did feel sorry—sorry for the man. Track's feelings weren't affected by Mob connections and the killings credited to Don Carlo Capezi in his early years, or Capezi's stranglehold on prostitution, gambling and drugs. It was simply human compassion for an old man who had lost his only daughter.

Unlike Capezi's other child, a son, Angelina Capezi had been unaffiliated with the family business, as unaffiliated as any child of a Mafia Don could be. From what Track had heard, she had been a nice girl. A kindergarten teacher who'd done volunteer work with a group devoted to the prevention of child abuse. She'd been a good kid, Track thought, who'd done nothing to deserve such a horrible death.

The medic with the strike force had said she had been repeatedly raped and abused before her throat had been slit.

The SPAS-12 rested against the tree stump beside him. Track looked at it for a moment. Three of the Israeli bandits had survived; two were wounded. He'd been tempted to use the SPAS and see that none had survived.

But he hadn't. "Good guys" weren't supposed to do that, he knew. And he was supposed to be a good guy, fighting for truth, justice and all the rest. But sometimes.... Track exhaled a cloud of gray smoke from his cigar and watched it catch on the wind and dissipate. "Shit," he murmured.

The knot of people in front of him was breaking up, and the overweight, short-legged Don Carlo Capezi began walking toward him.

Track stood up out of respect for the man's age and the man's grief.

"You are Major Track?"

"Yes."

"I want to thank you, sir," said the Don as he extended his right hand. Track thought for a moment, then took it. The handclasp was warm, dry, firm, but slightly trembling. The man's eyes were tear rimmed, but he held his head up. "Your courage and—" he gestured toward where George, Lew Wilson and the men of the strike force stood conversing with Sir Abner "—and the courageous acts of these other gentlemen in attempting to save the life of my daughter from those God-forsaken bastards warm an old man's heart in his time of grief. It will be a consolation to the girl's mother. I understand you are a man of the law, and because of some unfavorable publicity over the years I am mistakenly thought of as just the opposite. But there is a law greater than the law set forth in books and spoken of in courtrooms. Just as I swear vengeance against all the scum who are part of this gang that so cruelly violated my daughter and took her life, I also swear my undying friendship and respect for you and these other men. Please accept this small token, and when you look at it, think of me if I can be of help to you someday in your hour of need.'' And the Don reached into the right-hand vest pocket of his suit, removing something Track couldn't see. Capezi reached out and pressed the object into Track's palm. He nodded curtly, closing Track's fingers over the object, then turned and walked away, back toward the body of his daughter.

Track watched the old Don for a long moment, then opened his hand. He didn't know what to expect.

It looked to be made of sterling silver and was the size and shape of a business card. Engraved across it: Carlo G. Capezi—to my friend.

''Hmm,'' Track murmured. He looked away from the sterling-silver business card to the sad old man who had given it to him. Sometimes, Dan Track reflected, wealth, power—even the power of life and death—didn't mean a damned thing. . . .

THE FLORIDA SUN WARMED HIS LEGS beneath the swimming trunks, warmed them too much, and he slipped closer to the frosted-glass tabletop to get farther beneath the shade of the umbrella. Dan Track squinted at the reflected sunlight that radiated from the blue-watered pool like slivers of light seen through a prism.

He put on the sunglasses that rested beside the Cross pen on the table and stared at the yellow legal pad. It was empty of writing and had to be filled with the details of the destruction of the gang that had kidnapped the Don's daughter. He heard the sound of an aircraft overhead, but squinting skyward, he saw only the brilliant reflection of sunlight from the plane's body. He imagined the jet to be the one he should have been on, taking him overseas and eventually to Desiree Goth's home in Switzerland. He had called her at 2:00 A.M. just before going to sleep, awakening her. Sounding half asleep, she had whispered, ''I love you—are you coming?'' He'd answered that he'd been forced by circumstance to delay the time together he had promised her, but only by a few days. There had been a long silence, and then she had begun to tell him things, private things, and after a long time they had said goodbye and hung up. He had lain awake, staring into the darkness for hours after that, remembering the blackness of her hair and the surreal blueness of her eyes.

Track looked toward the pool at the sound of a splash and saw his nephew George break the surface of the water and begin to swim the length of the pool in long, even strokes. Behind him, he heard Sir Abner Chesterton. "Writer's block, Dan?"

Track looked toward Chesterton. With his thinning hair and rapier slimness, the coordinator for the Consortium looked out of place in swimming trunks. He sat down at the chair opposite Track, in the full sunlight; his pale body seemed to redden the instant the sun touched it. "I said, writer's block?"

Track picked up the pen. "No—wishful thinking."

"We should have all the legal paperwork cared for within another day, two at the most, and then you can be on your way."

Track looked away from Sir Abner, down to a white scar on his left arm, the reminder of another battle with another enemy—Johannes Krieger. "Hell, after what we've just been through, I need a vacation."

"I think it greatly to your credit, Dan, that savagery can still affront you," Sir Abner said.

Track cleared his throat. "You mean the way—"

"The girl was killed," Sir Abner finished for him. "Yes, precisely that. By the way, your friend Lew Wilson's data has only confirmed what we suspected. This Malina gang is reaching large proportions in the United States. It's not a terrorist element but a new criminal society, like the Mafia. Rather ironic, actually—Don Carlo Capezi being so horribly victimized by something so similar to his own organization. When you fly off to Europe and the arms of your Miss Goth, I'm afraid I'll be flying to Jerusalem to meet with representatives of various Israeli police agencies, the Israeli defense forces and the Mossad. They've pledged whatever cooperation is needed to help us crack this gang, to smash them. Many of the Malina members fled Israel after committing major crimes there, as well, and the Israeli authorities feel more than a little responsible—unofficially, of course—for the training that has made some of them so deadly."

"It's not the first time soldiers have gone bad," Track said. "It's nothing the Israelis should take personally."

"But there are a lot of people who feel Israel is too much the favored nation already," Chesterton responded. "And the presence in the United States of a largely Israeli gang, well organized, heavily armed, mercilessly brutal, won't help matters like that."

Track only nodded in reply.

Sir Abner continued. "When you get back, it's been the decision of the Consortium that you, George and I should devote all our efforts to tracking down the central leadership of these people, tracking them down and putting as much a stop to their activities as possible. As we've discussed before, kidnappings seem to be one of their favored activities—and they almost always murder their victims. At the moment, their crimes represent nickel-and-dime level crime to us—I believe that's the correct Americanism?"

Dan Track nodded.

"Such a remark sounds callous, I know, but I also perceive their activities as leading to larger crimes. If they can be nipped in the bud, we may save ourselves considerable difficulty later."

"You're not going to nip these guys in the bud, Sir Abner. They're tough."

"Then," said Sir Abner as his right eyebrow cocked and his brow furrowed, "we shall have to try even harder, shan't we?"

Track leaned forward and laughed. He slapped Sir Abner on the thigh, saying, "Yes, I suppose we will!"

Track stood up, stepped out of his rubber thongs and walked toward the pool. George was just climbing out. Dan Track dived in. He considered the Olympic-sized pool and the expensive rented house at his disposal; it was in some respects the American dream. Sunshine and the accessories of wealth. But he would rather have been walking a snowy Alpine trail—with Desiree Goth.

4

Josh Culhane stood on the porch of his house at Lake Lanier, near Gainesville, in northeastern Georgia, and watched Mary Frances Mulrooney at the water's edge. The sunset was just beginning, and the surface of the enormous man-made lake was flecked with gold. As Culhane watched, he thought about how Fanny, as he called her, had kept her apartment in Athens, Georgia, calling it "an escape valve for both of us," but she had moved in with him. In the peaceful atmosphere of Lake Lanier, she had been concluding her latest book, *Occult Murmurs*.

He shook his head. He hadn't thought that two writers could exist together in such close confines without doing serious injury to each other, let alone writers who were also lovers. His own books, The Takers series, were a far cry from her work.

Sean Dodge, the action-adventure hero he'd created, paid the bills and allowed him to lead an exciting life. Culhane considered himself a distinctly unsedentary writer and always tried to experience firsthand the exotic and sometimes dangerous adventures that found their way into the Sean Dodge novels.

He'd only recently returned from Latin America, where he'd faced enough danger to last for a while. Fanny had said he was like an addict who had got his fix. Now he was looking forward to the relative peacefulness of a writers' conference his publisher was hosting in Las Vegas the next day. His only fear was that the conference might be too boring. But it would give him a good opportunity to spend some time with his old friend

Ed Morrison and catch up on events. And that, too, would be all right.

Culhane turned his attention back to Fanny Mulrooney. She was jumping rope, and her dark hair bounced as she moved. As he started down the steps leading from the porch, he noticed that it wasn't a rope she was jumping after all but a ten-foot bullwhip he'd recently received from a supplier. He was always experimenting with weapons and gadgets for the fearless Sean Dodge to use against some new arch villain. As he approached her more closely, he could see the gray-green color of her eyes in the sunset, the radiance of health that glowed from her face with the exertion.

He watched her for a moment longer, lighting a Pall Mall with his red disposable Bic. He inhaled, picked a piece of tobacco from his lower lip with his right index finger, then exhaled the gray smoke as he spoke. "Fanny—you realize what that is?"

She didn't stop jumping—she was doing it backward now—but she answered him in a breathless voice, "Yeah, it's—it's a bullwhip. I know what it is, Josh!"

"But Cattle Baron Leather didn't send it to me for you to jump rope with. In the next Takers, Sean Dodge runs up against a terrorist who uses a bullwhip and then Dodge has to face him. They duel with the whips. So I've got to learn how to use it."

"You use it to jump rope, silly." She laughed, finally stopping, exhaling hard, leaning against a tree. She threw him the whip. "Can you jump rope?"

"Some other time—I have to leave tomorrow for Las Vegas, and I don't feel like going to that writers' conference with both ankles in casts."

Mulrooney laughed. "You won't break anything."

"If you want to jump rope, why aren't you using a rope?"

"Oh, sure, maybe the rappeling rope in the trunk of your car—what is it, fifty feet long?"

Culhane didn't answer her, heeling out his cigarette, looking at the whip.

"Do you know how to make it do that cracking sound?" Fanny Mulrooney asked him.

"Yeah, I know how to make it do that cracking sound."

"All right, fine, let's see you do it—go on."

"Not now—"

"You can't do it, huh?"

"Yeah, I can do it."

"I never saw you practice with it—when did you practice with it?"

"Before I left for Latin America. The whip came while you were investigating that UFO sighting in Colorado."

"So, okay, then—make the whip crack for me, Josh."

Culhane shook his head. "What are you making for dinner?" he asked.

"Instant coffee—so go crack the whip."

Josh Culhane didn't say anything. The whip was coiled in his right hand. He snaked it back behind him to its full ten-foot length, then quickly drew the whip forward and up. The whip curled in the air over his head and behind him as his right hand and arm moved forward. He flexed his right wrist and the whip snaked forward. An audible crack sounded on the air as the fall at the tip broke the sound barrier. He did it a few more times, then gathered up the whip into three loose coils. He looked at Mulrooney. "Well?"

"Pretty good. What else can you do with it?"

Culhane flicked his right arm back, the whip behind him, then snaked it forward. The fall and the shaft of the whip wrapped around Mulrooney's bare legs just at the ankles, but gently. He walked toward her, slackening the whip. "How'd you like that?"

"Aw—you know that kinky stuff turns me on," and she leaned up and kissed him hard on the mouth. "So much so that I'll make you some dinner," and as he grabbed for her, she slipped from his fingers and was gone, running up toward the house.

Josh Culhane closed his eyes, laughing. . . .

SHE'D MADE STEAKS, hers rare and bleeding and his medium, and eggs, hers an omelet with diced green peppers and onions and sour-cream salad dressing, his sunny-side up and barely warmed. She'd made drinks, pouring dark rum from a one-liter bottle into the bourbon glasses Culhane had called Doc Hollidays ever since he had been a kid and watched Kirk Douglas as the consumptive, gunfighting Georgia dentist. She'd made coffee, the decaffeinated instant Nescafé he liked. And they had gone to bed and made love—they'd done that together, and he'd liked it better than the coffee, the rum, the eggs or the steak.

She lay in the crook of his right arm now, her head against his chest. The darkness in their room was softened by the light of a full moon. "Why don't you just stay in Las Vegas with me?" Culhane asked. "The writers' conference is only going to be two-and-a-half days—and then we can chase after your Seven Golden Cities of Cibola together. You putting that in your next book?"

"No, my next book is about warrior women."

"Warrior women?" Culhane repeated.

"Yeah, warrior women. You know, like the Amazons."

"Wonder Woman?"

"No, the Greek legends and everything—like that."

"Then why are you looking for seven golden cities that supposedly don't exist—in New Mexico yet?" Culhane asked her.

"In Arizona—on the New Mexico border. The legend has persisted for decades that the Zuni Indians had built seven cities of gold."

"Let me ask you a question," Culhane murmured,

shifting his shoulder under her head. "Do all Zuni Indians own Rolls-Royces or Bentleys?"

"Of course they don't. That's a dumb question!"

"But if they have seven golden cities, why don't they just take down part of a bedroom wall and buy Rolls-Royces and Bentleys?"

"Shut up," she said as she laughed.

"Seriously, I don't want you out in some desert running around looking for golden housing developments all by yourself."

"I can take care of myself very well, thank you," she answered. "You taught me, remember?"

"You can't shoot worth a damn past thirty feet—"

"Poor quality of teaching I had."

"Can't you wait two-and-a-half days?"

"That old prospector needs me out there tomorrow night. He's going to meet me not too far from the airport, and then you can join us after you get through in Vegas—no big deal."

Culhane exhaled hard, half blowing in her ear. She looked up at him, kissing him lightly on the cheek. He told her, "You be careful, really careful. Don't let some old loony take you out in the desert for—"

"For what?" and she wriggled around, looking at him, leaning on his chest.

"Move your elbow," he said. "Anybody ever tell you you've got sharp elbows?"

"For what?" Fanny Mulrooney repeated. "What's he going to take me out in the desert for?"

Culhane drew her closer to him, rolling her over, rolling over then on top of her, slipping between her thighs. She laughed, whispering into his left ear, "You sure you've got enough energy to do it again? I mean, after all, you told me how tired you—" And she sucked in her breath in a little scream. "That must be why you ate so much tonight! You really are a growing boy," she said as she laughed.

5

He wanted to do this especially right.

The orders, despite the usual insulation route, would have come directly from the old Don himself, Mike Pirelli guessed. And if the operation went as smooth as a baby's backside, the Don would know about it. If it didn't, he'd know about that, too, Pirelli told himself soberly.

The radio buzzed in his ear and he adjusted the earpiece, then picked up the handset, turning away from the street traffic on the driver's side of the Cadillac Seville and making certain the sidewalk was deserted before he spoke. "This is Lucky—come back to me."

He'd picked the code name "Lucky" for himself. If the operation went well, that was just what he would be, and he smiled, thinking about it.

The voice of Dennis Strackmann came back. "Lucky—this is Tinfish. Phase one is go all the way—repeat, go all the way. Come back."

"Tinfish—Lucky here. Reading you loud and clear. Move into position as ordered. Lucky out." He reached down to the CB under the dash, picked up the microphone and depressed the talk button. The CB dial was set on Channel Fourteen. "This is Lucky," he said into the microphone. "Good Christian men rejoice. I repeat, good Christian men rejoice." He'd come up with the code phrase himself, thinking it was particularly appropriate since they were about to kill two Israelis and Israelis weren't Christian. Pirelli considered that he was a Christian. It was said that the Don never trusted a man

unless he made confession every Saturday night and
Mass every Sunday.

Pirelli thought about that for a moment as he hung up
the CB microphone; going to church did give him a
good feeling. He flipped back the sport coat on the seat
beside him. The MAC-10 with the sound suppressor
beneath the jacket also gave him a good feeling.

He covered up the .45 ACP submachine gun and
checked his sideview mirror as he fired the Seville's ignition. There was very little traffic at 2:00 A.M., and he
turned into the street. He felt like whistling, but
couldn't decide on any special tune.

As HE STOOD beside Lew Wilson, yawning because it was
just after two in the morning, George flexed his shoulders under the Bianchi Scorpio shoulder rig that carried
his new Smith & Wesson Model 469. As a result of the
experience he'd gained with Track and the Consortium,
he had decided that he needed a second steady handgun
to complement his Colt Combat Government .45.

"You tired?" Wilson asked.

"Yeah, but I've never helped with a prisoner transfer
before, and I figured I could use the experience."

Wilson shrugged and nodded. "Tell you what. I've
done this before, so why don't you join FDLE so you
can represent the State of Florida here, and I'll go home
to bed."

George laughed. "Well, not right this minute." Then
he turned the corners of his mouth down in displeasure.
"You really think Carlo Capezi is going to try for these
guys?"

"The Israeli we had in the hospital got an embolism
from his IV tube—so, yeah, I think he's got something
planned between here and the airport. In the old days,
before he started building his new image, they used to
call the old Don by his nickname."

George didn't say anything.

Wilson went on, "'Crazy' Capezi. Can you see a nickname like that? But that's what they called him, because he'd do anything that had to be done. The story goes that when he got off the boat from Sicily, he'd already committed his first murder in the United States. Apparently there was a guy from a rival gang on the boat, and Capezi broke his neck and tossed him into the water off Ellis Island. I don't know if it's true or not, but it makes a good story," and Wilson laughed.

They bided their time by the emergency-room exit of the small prison hospital while the FBI brought the two Israelis from their cells. They had left Dan Track and Sir Abner Chesterton waiting in a rented LTD across the street from the county jail.

George shrugged, yawning again as he heard footsteps from the other side of the portholed swinging doors. It would be the FBI and the two kidnappers. George Beegh asked himself a question: Why was he up at 2:00 A.M., one gun on his hip, another under his arm, trying to guard two men he would just as soon strangle with his bare hands for what they had done?

There wasn't any answer to it, but he knew what Wilson would say if he was asked—they were innocent men until they were proved guilty.

George lit a Winston as the doors opened. He couldn't forget what the kidnappers had done to Angelina Capezi. He didn't want to forget.

DAN TRACK OPENED HIS EYES, feeling something jabbing at him, hearing Sir Abner Chesterton's voice. "Dan— wake up, they're coming!"

Track looked around, raising himself in the front seat of the LTD. He rubbed his eyes, running both hands through his hair. The visor in front of him was turned down against the glare of a streetlamp and he studied himself in the vanity mirror. His mustache needed trimming. "What's happening?" he asked, trying to sound good-natured rather than angry at being awakened.

"George, Lew Wilson and the FBI team are coming through the emergency-room exit with the two prisoners."

Track shook his head, yawning. "Right—George and Lew ride in the back of the ambulance with the two kidnappers, and two FBI guys drive the ambulance. We follow them, and there's a carload of FBI agents ahead of them."

"Are you attempting to demonstrate how wide awake you are?"

Track looked at Sir Abner and grinned. "Yeah, well, just trying to remind myself what's happening." Track twisted around in his seat, checking the rear seat where his SPAS-12 and an M-16 for Sir Abner rested beneath a blanket. The blanket also hid a very special attaché case. He shook his head, yawning, pushing up the vanity-mirrored visor and opening the glove compartment. He took the Trapper Scorpion from it and replaced the little .45 in the Alessi inside-the-pants holster beside his right kidney. It was comfortable to wear, but no holster rig was comfortable to sleep in, except some of the shoulder holsters. He nudged at the Metalife Custom L-Frame under his bomber jacket with his left upper arm and elbow and shifted his shoulders under the harness.

Track gazed past Sir Abner Chesterton and watched as George and Lew Wilson stepped up the concrete platform and disappeared inside the ambulance. There was an audible thud in the nighttime stillness as the ambulance doors closed. He heard one, then another engine come to life. Then the unmarked interagency motor-pool car started away from the platform, with the ambulance right behind it. Track watched the two vehicles move across the tarred parking lot toward the eight-foot-high cyclone fence that walled in the prison hospital from the street.

The LTD's engine purred to life as Sir Abner said, "I assume you prefer that I drive?"

Track yawned again and laughed. "I don't care either way, but I wouldn't ride with a guy as wide awake as I am."

The prison gates opened and the FBI sedan and the ambulance passed through. Sir Abner turned around, looking into the street, then steered the LTD into a U-turn, crossing the four traffic lanes and pulling in behind the ambulance.

Track found one of his Cuesta-Rey Six-Ts, guillotined the tip, then began searching for his Zippo. Sir Abner was speaking. "Do you really suppose Capezi will attempt to have these two men murdered while under the protective custody of the FBI?"

"You bet I do," Track said as he reached into the back seat for the SPAS. "And if I were the old Don and those assholes did to my daughter what they did to his, hell—I'd do it, too." Dan Track worked the magazine cutoff button, sliding one of the Federal Super Slugs into the chamber of the SPAS. "He'll do it between here and the airport. I'd lay money on it." And Track let the shotgun's bolt slide forward with a resounding click.

6

"Step on it!" Track cranked down the side window of the LTD, feeling the comparative coolness of the night air push at his face; he was suddenly completely awake. A car had fallen in behind them, and another trailed behind it. He looked back again. The cars had increased their speed and were matching the LTD. Track leaned back inside, snatching up the hand microphone for the radio. "This is Track. Two unfriendlies coming up fast. Over!" There was nothing but a long droning whistle. "This is Dan. George—Lew—anybody!"

The droning whistle continued to reply, but no voice.

"They must be jamming the radio," Sir Abner whispered hoarsely, but Track could barely hear him.

Track nodded, working off the carrying safety to the right of the SPAS's trigger guard, leaving only the quick-employment safety set. "Pull up beside the ambulance and match their speed," he said to Sir Abner.

"Right!"

The LTD's engine growled softly as the transmission kicked. Track felt the car shudder slightly and watched the shops and light posts that lined the street on both sides whip by.

Track looked behind them. The two cars were coming up fast. He looked ahead. The LTD was nearly even with the ambulance, and from his vantage point Track could see three more cars ahead, only one of them the FBI sedan.

They were crossing an all-but-abandoned intersection in a derelict part of the city of Miami as two more cars closed in from the left side of the intersection and joined the assault force behind the ambulance.

As Sir Abner pulled even with the ambulance, Track shouted to the FBI driver, "They've got us boxed in— radio's gone!"

The man nodded, and the ambulance pulled ahead. Sir Abner dropped back, turning in behind the ambulance.

A voice boomed over a loudspeaker from one of the cars behind them. "We want only the two Israelis! Pull over, let them out and drive off, and we will leave you alone."

Track pegged the voice as coming from the lead car of the three behind them.

"Hold her steady, Sir Abner," Track shouted, as he pushed the SPAS out the side window and pulled the trigger. The car behind them stopped dead and skidded as first one, then a second car following it slammed into its rear end. The gas tank erupted and tongues of orange flame licked the night.

Track tucked back inside the LTD.

"Sir Abner, get us up even with the ambulance again, fast."

As the LTD accelerated Track saw that the men in the cars in front of the ambulance had started to exchange fire with the agents in the FBI sedan. Behind him, one of the cars that had joined in at the intersection had navigated the burning wreckage of the original assault cars and was closing fast.

The LTD was nearly even with the ambulance as Track fed another slug into the SPAS's magazine so he'd have a full eight rounds plus the one in the chamber.

Track shouted up to the ambulance driver, "When I take out that last car, bootleg it as fast as you can and stick close to me!"

"All right, but how the hell do I know you know what you're doing?"

"Would a face like this lie?" Track said as he tucked back inside, commanding Sir Abner, "Drop back again and when I get that car riding drag, get this bus turned around superquick."

"Right, tell me when."

Track nodded, eyeing the car behind them, then glanced at Sir Abner again. "Do you know Miami?" he asked.

"As a matter of fact, I do rather well, Dan. I spent a good deal of time here in 1974 and again in 1977," Chesterton replied.

"Great," said Track. "As soon as we peel off, find us a big broad street that has a long straight stretch."

"Right."

Track thrust the SPAS-12 through the window again, firing left-handed. The pursuit car swerved, and Track brought the SPAS on line and pulled the trigger. The windshield of the Mafia car shattered, and the car careered wildly, out of control. Track watched as it bounced up over the curb, crushed a blue-and-white mailbox and rammed a fire hydrant, turning loose a gusher. A smile crossed Track's lips. "How about that real quick turn, Sir Abner?" he asked.

Chesterton laughed. "Hold on, Dan!"

The big LTD screamed to a stop, skidding forward. Track braced himself just in time to keep from being hurtled into the windshield.

Chesterton pushed the gearshift lever two notches to the left and stomped on the gas. The LTD's rear wheels squealed and sent up billows of white smoke as the car went into a high-speed reverse. As Sir Abner jerked the wheel of the LTD, Track rammed more of the slug loads into the magazine of the SPAS. The LTD screeched to a halt, the front end swerving around almost 180 degrees. Track's stomach pulled with the motion as the car shuddered to a stop, pointing in the opposite direction. The car hesitated for an instant, and then Track was shoved back against the seat back by the force of the sudden acceleration as Sir Abner brought his foot down hard on the gas.

Track looked behind them. Both the ambulance and the FBI sedan had bootlegged onto the other side of the street, jumped the curb and turned to follow them.

"Slow us down, drop back and be ready to fly, Sir Abner," Track snapped, feeling the rented Ford lurch under him. He glanced at Chesterton as the Ford came even with the ambulance; the FBI point car was tailgating it. Behind them, three pursuit cars steadily closed the distance. Track figured they had bought fifteen seconds at the outside.

Track leaned into the back seat and brought the attaché case forward, working the locks, opening the lid. Inside was a Walther MPK, the short version of the Walther submachine gun. In the case, along with the subgun, were four 32-round magazines. Track took one of these and rammed it up the magazine well, then set the subgun down on the LTD's front seat beside Chesterton.

"Remember how much you liked the Walther MPK, Sir Abner? Well, now you're going to get a chance to use it. We're going to throw this car out as a block against some of the pursuit cars. You use the Walther. I'll use the SPAS."

Track was loading the SPAS-12 when Chesterton said suddenly, "That broad street you wanted—how about the MacArthur Causeway over the bay into Miami Beach?"

"A bridge—perfect. Hit it." The LTD was beside the ambulance, and Track shouted out his window. "Follow us onto the causeway up ahead. When we peel off, drive like hell!"

"Right," the FBI agent behind the wheel of the ambulance shouted back.

"Sir Abner, how soon—" Track began.

"We'll reach the causeway in another minute, perhaps less," Chesterton responded, anticipating the question.

"We might not have a minute. Step on it—" Track urged. There was a low hum from the motor, which grew to a roar as the LTD surged ahead.

Track looked behind them. Gunfire was coming from the passenger windows of the three remaining mob cars that now blocked the entire street behind them like a wall. In the distance he could see the Mars lights of police vehicles responding to the gunfire. But the mafioso vehicles weren't turning off.

As he turned to face the front and readied the SPAS, he could see the signs for the MacArthur Causeway, the black expanse of the bay and, beyond it, the lights of Miami Beach. "Once we're on the causeway," Track said to Chesterton, "drop back even with the FBI car and let the ambulance and it pass you. Then get this thing turned around to block the road laterally from my side. You get out quick and get away from the car and start using that Walther subgun. I'll get out on their side and let them have it with the SPAS." He'd loaded the SPAS-12 this time with 2-3/4 double 0 buck. He worked the magazine cutoff button and chambered a solitary slug load. "I'll keep the buckshot as a surprise," Track murmured, not knowing if Chesterton was still listening.

As they hit the causeway, the LTD made a violent lurch to the right and bounced, then dropped. Track felt the vehicle shudder around him, then accelerate. As he turned to look behind him, he saw the ambulance turn onto the causeway. The FBI car was right behind it.

Within seconds, the first of the three pursuit cars was on the bridge, with the other two coming fast behind it, sticking to the right-hand lanes. In the middle of the roadway was a divider, too big for a passenger car to jump without breaking an axle.

"Start dropping back, Sir Abner," Track commanded.

Chesterton nodded, and Track could feel the Ford starting to slow as first the ambulance passed them, then the FBI car. In the rear of the ambulance, its doors wide open and flapping like useless wings with each bump and jar, he could see George, the little Smith 469 clasped in both fists, and beside him Lew Wilson, his Beretta 92-SB flashing fire. Both men were backlit by the light from inside the ambulance.

"Now, Sir Abner—turn right now!" Track yelled.

Track steeled himself, anchoring the subgun to the seat beside Sir Abner with his left hand as the brakes screeched and his body lurched forward, despite the brace he'd taken with his legs. His right hand went out just in time to save his head from slamming against the dashboard. The big LTD twisted to the right, its rear end fishtailing, and the car skidded laterally to a halt.

Track shoved the Walther subgun toward Sir Abner; Chesterton's door was already open.

Track slid out on the passenger side, his right index finger pushing the combat safety forward from the trigger guard, then snapping back against the SPAS's trigger as he fired the solitary slug load into the grill of the lead car of the mob pursuit force.

The car screamed to a stop, fluid pouring from beneath the hood, a gusher of steam rising through the shot-out grill, as a second mob car clipped the rear end.

Track was moving, half throwing himself, half rolling across the hood of the LTD, firing the SPAS again as he came out of the roll and slid down behind the engine compartment of the Ford beside the left-front fender. The buckshot sprayed into the windshield of the third mob car as it slowed to avoid hitting the other two.

Track ran toward one of the bridge supports, hearing the light chatter of Sir Abner Chesterton's Walther MPK subgun from behind him. He tucked back beside the bridge support, as a fusillade of submachine gunfire from the occupants of the three mob cars hammered into the metal pillar. The whine of police sirens skipped across the bay, and in the distance, at the west end of the causeway, he could see the flashing lights of at least four police cars; the cars were closing fast in both the incoming and outgoing lanes. Track shouldered the SPAS, firing again and again, shattering the glass from the body of the nearest of the mob cars. As men ran from behind it, Sir Abner's subgun sprayed into them, cutting them down. Track fired out the SPAS, slicing a Mafia subgunner almost in two at the waist with a double dose of buckshot.

Track rammed more of the buckshot up the magazine tube, chambering a round, and ran back toward the LTD. He worked the trigger of the SPAS as he moved, and one of the Mafia killers went down, then a second and third.

He looked behind him, loading the last few rounds he had for the SPAS as he did. Sir Abner was running from cover, his Walther MPK spitting neat 3-round bursts at the surviving Mafia gunmen.

With three rounds in the SPAS, Track pushed up from cover, firing toward the farthest of the mob cars, shattering the windshield, skipping pellets off the hood of the car. One of the Mafia triggermen screamed and fell back, hands held to his face, blood seeping from between the fingers. Track fired again, blowing out a side window in a car. A man firing a subgun darted from beside the car and Track squeezed the trigger on the SPAS, blowing the man's legs out from under him. The subgun fired wildly as the man collapsed in agony.

Track slung the empty SPAS behind him, muzzle down, his right hand snatching the Metalife Custom L-Frame from the Alessi shoulder rig. The .357's trigger twitched twice, putting the knee-capped mob subgunner away with two rounds into the torso. The police cars screamed to a stop, and uniformed officers poured from them as a voice over a PA system shouted, "Throw down your weapons—you are under arrest!"

To his left, from the farthest mob car, Track heard the sound of a subgun and instinctively wheeled toward it. Sir Abner's Walther MPK chattered from behind him, and the mobster's body danced with the hits. Track raised the L-Frame in a solid two-handed grip and double-actioned it four times. The subgunner sank to his knees, his body splotched with red, riddled with bullets. The subgun made a tinny sound as it clattered to the bridge surface.

"Drop that gun!" one of the police officers shouted. Track looked down the bridge to the police cars. Revolvers and riot shotguns were trained on him. Slowly he raised his hands—he'd let Chesterton recite the litany of who they were—but he didn't drop the L-Frame.

He could hear a radio crackling from one of the mob cars. Somebody was calling for someone code named Lucky—or maybe that was the guy's nickname. Track shrugged it off. None of the Mafia hitmen lived; it was unlikely anyone of them could have been called "Lucky."

7

Josh Culhane set down the Atlanta newspaper on the empty seat beside him. The flight was going on to Los Angeles, and maybe somebody would want to read it. He watched as the passengers choked the aisle, ducking back a little as the woman who had been sitting beside him opened the overhead compartment and searched for something. Culhane looked at his watch. It was 3:00 P.M. eastern time—noon in Las Vegas. He shrugged and picked up the newspaper again, looking once more at the story about the Miami shoot-out. Sorting through the article, it appeared to him as obvious that Crazy Carlo Capezi had ordered the hit on the two surviving Israelis who had been involved in the kidnapping and murder of his daughter.

The newspaper linked the Israelis with a group called the Malina, and according to the newspaper account, one of the Israelis had been slightly wounded by flying debris in the chase; the other was shaken but all right. It sounded like quite a chase, he thought, through half of Miami and almost out to Miami Beach.

"Hmm," he muttered, taking off his wire-framed glasses and rubbing at the bridge of his nose. He decided to add the article to his files, and after folding his glasses into the breast pocket of his sport coat, he took the knife blade on his money clip and cut out the article from the paper.

Josh Culhane fed the article into the expandable file section of his old Samsonite attaché case, then closed the case and left it on his lap. The aisle of the 727 was still too crowded to bother trying to get up, let alone make for the aircraft's door. He thought about the Israelis. He had read various articles about the Malina, had been told various things from friends in law enforcement agencies and in the press. No one seemed quite certain when the gang had organized, but in many ways it was similar to the Sicilian Mafia that had exported itself to the United States around the turn of the century.

Culhane thought over what he knew about the Israeli mob. Most members were veterans of the Israeli defense forces, men and women trained to kill as efficiently as possible. That alone made them formidable opponents. Now the Malina were using their skills, honed in warfare, to create a major criminal organization in the United States. The police had had little success in stopping them and apparently no success in penetrating their organization.

Culhane smiled. The crowd in the aisle was thinning as he stood and ducked beneath the still-open overhead compartment panel. As he worked the stiffness out of his legs he thought that the Israeli gang might make a wonderful new enemy for Sean Dodge, his nearly invincible action-adventure hero. He was already starting on one level of consciousness to come up with a title. Some authors titled books after writing them. He never had. He reached into the overhead compartment and took down the tan Burberry trench coat he had carried on to the aircraft. On still another level, he was already fashioning a plot. Since the gang was partially Israeli, it would be wise to involve an Israeli with Sean Dodge in battling them—perhaps a lusciously attractive, dark-eyed Mossad agent with sweat glistening in her cleavage as she and Sean Dodge stormed one of the gang strongholds.

"Hmm," Culhane murmured again, getting his stuff bag down. He slung the bag over his left shoulder, then the trench coat across the same shoulder, before picking up his attaché case in his right hand. The aisle was nearly clear, and now was the time to hurry. . . .

HE COULD SEE THE COVER in his mind's eye—perhaps a Star of David dripping blood, with Sean Dodge and the dark-haired, voluptuous Mossad agent running from inside it, submachine guns firing. He waited beside the rotating luggage carousel, looking for his suit bag and suitcase. The suitcase would be easy to find, so easy to find it was theft bait for any sticky-fingered person who might happen by. It carried the mandatory red tag on the handle that read, in bold letters, Firearms.

So sometimes the law is stupid, he thought, almost verbalizing it. He saw the suit bag and snatched it from the carousel, still looking for the specially marked suitcase. He glanced at his watch—it was nearly twelve-thirty. The first actual meeting at the author conference would be dinner at seven that night. That would be ten according to his body.

He yawned, murmuring, "Aw, shit—" Then he noticed a woman turn to stare at him, grinned and said, "Sorry," and looked back to the carousel. He saw his case, its little red tag twitching with the motion of the luggage dispenser. He walked around and plucked it off the gleaming aluminum of the carousel, instantly ripping the firearms tag from the handle. No point in advertising himself as a target.

He felt like a pack mule as he started away from the luggage area. Half a minute later he set down the suitcase and attaché case to stuff the red firearms tag in a trash receptacle, then picked up the two cases and started out.

The Las Vegas sun made the walk seem doubly arduous by the time he reached the butt end of the line waiting for taxicabs. He set down his luggage, resigned to the wait, half-surprised the airport management hadn't installed slot machines for people to use while they stood in line. Slot machines had been the first thing to greet him as he had entered the terminal, followed by the voices of Las Vegas entertainers on prerecorded messages over the PA system, welcoming passengers. He moved up two spaces and waited beneath the sun....

As THE YELLOW TAXICAB pulled into the circular drive that ran between the low steps leading into the Vegas Crown and the fountains with naked little cast-concrete bodies facing the street, Culhane assessed the hotel itself. The building rose twenty-eight stories, with a four-story glass atrium at the front. Two grotesque chandelierlike appendages flanked the front doors. The style was strictly prefab drab, and Culhane wondered if the hotel had been erected or simply injection molded.

A red-coated doorman was reaching for the door of the cab as Culhane stepped out and walked to the rear of the car, where the driver was taking the luggage out of the trunk. He paid the driver seven dollars and some change, adding on the remainder of the ten-dollar bill as a tip. "I need a receipt," he told the cabbie.

"I don't got a pen," the man replied, looking straight at Culhane.

Culhane reached into the pocket of his sport coat, sighing as he handed over a Bic pen. "Here—and keep it."

"Sure thing, pal." The driver nodded as he slammed the trunk lid closed, leaving Culhane's luggage on the driveway. He took the pen and walked back to the front of his cab.

The doorman was hovering. Culhane slipped him a dollar, "Get me a bellman, huh?"

"I'll see if I can locate someone, sir," the man said as he turned and walked up the hotel steps.

"Aw, wonderful," Culhane snarled.

The cabdriver stood in front of Culhane, holding up a slip of paper and grinning. "Hey—hope ya win a bundle, pal!" he said.

Culhane pocketed the receipt and nodded. "Thanks, but I never gamble."

No bellman had arrived, and the doorman was no-where in sight, so Culhane reached down for his luggage, arranging his burdens so they could be carried, then started up the long, low steps. At the top of the steps, a woman was coming through the automatic doors, and he stepped aside for her, almost getting clipped as the doors swung out. He walked through two sets of doors and into the hotel lobby. Someone had liked the color of blood—the carpet, the drapes, even the face of the long front desk was red. Gold trim was splashed everywhere, and the effect was genuine Las Vegas kitsch, Culhane thought. Four floors above his head was a red brocade ceiling with gold edges. Chandeliers carved of genuine plastic crystal, he guessed, were suspended by gold chains from the ceiling.

To his right, out of sight of the windows leading to the street so no one could tell what time of day it was while he gambled away his life savings, were the tables, the ma-chines and the people, sending up a hum like a swarm of insects as they put their money down or dropped their coins in the slots.

Culhane started for the section of front desk nearest him and set down his luggage. "I'm Josh Culhane," he announced. "My publisher made a reservation for me."

The man smiled, looked away and tapped a few keys on a computer terminal. "Yes, Mr. Culhane—we have your reservation. You're booked into room 808," and he looked up from the terminal, smiled and said quite formally, "I'm a great fan of your books, sir."

"Well, thanks." Culhane felt himself grin. "The Takers, huh?"

"No—I'm afraid I just never could get into those at

all. It was the series you used to write—sorry, the name escapes me.''

Culhane shrugged, feeling his jaw set. "Yeah, the name escapes me, too. Can you get me a bellman to hike this stuff to my room?''

"I'll have a bellman take your things, sir, but your room won't be ready for approximately thirty minutes.''

"Wonderful." Culhane smiled.

"I might suggest trying your luck, Mr. Culhane—" and he gestured across the lobby into the casino.

Culhane exhaled hard. "I drink, I smoke, I dance, I tell dirty jokes. I don't go to church very often, but I don't gamble.''

"Oh.''

"Josh! Josh Culhane!''

Culhane heard his name being shouted and looked to his right, where a familiar figure stalked toward him— well over six feet tall, with a shock of white hair falling down in his eyes and a drooping Poncho Villa mustache, white like the hair. Culhane had recognized the voice. "Ed Morrison! They actually got you to come to this thing?'' Culhane looked at the older man. Morrison's high forehead was seamed with lines, looking like a topographic map.

"Yeah, well, Thom needed the benefit of my experience,'' Morrison said as he took Culhane's hand, pumping it warmly. Then Morrison leaned toward him and confided, "Maybe he figured an old pro like me should be here just in case there was trouble,'' and Morrison leaned back and winked. He released Culhane's hand and gestured toward his bags on the red carpeted floor. "They making you wait for your room, too?''

"Yeah. Wonderful, huh?''

"These people can't do shit,'' and Morrison turned to the desk clerk. "Son, Mr. Culhane and I will be in the bar while we're waiting for rooms that should have been ready a couple of hours ago, and all the drinks are going on our room tabs, but the house is going to pick them up.''

"I, ah, I can't authorize that sort of thing, Mr. Morrison—'' the clerk began.

"Well, then, sonny—you just talk to somebody who can. They got complaints, tell them to take it up with old Ed Morrison.'' Then Morrison clapped Culhane on the shoulder. "Come on, Josh, the hotel's buying!''

Culhane tried shrinking into his Florsheims, but it didn't work. Mentally he shrugged, snatching up the suitcase containing his firearms. He grinned at the desk clerk. "Why don't you have the bellman put the rest of these someplace safe. I'll take this one myself.''

"Very good, Mr. Culhane,'' and the desk clerk with great flair whacked the palm of his hand down on a bell and shouted, "Front!''

Culhane fell into step with Morrison and felt the pressure of Morrison's right hand against his left forearm slow him up as a wedge of five men cut in front of them and disappeared toward the elevator banks. "That's Joe Capezi,'' said Morrison, "son and heir of Crazy Carlo Capezi. His daddy and I go way back—he used to commit the crimes and I used to cover them when I was a crime reporter with the Chicago papers. The old man owns the casino—at least on paper he does,'' and Morrison began to walk again. Culhane looked back at the group of men and tried to pick out Capezi.

"These days the mobsters dress real good,'' Morrison continued, "but not too good. And they look like executives with computer outfits—hell.''

Culhane lit a Pall Mall with his lighter. "Well, I guess even the mob changes with the times, Ed,'' he said.

"Outside, they change. Inside, they never change. Come on, let's get that drink.''

Culhane said nothing. . . .

THE BAR WAS ON A SMALL MEZZANINE three steps up from the casino floor and overlooking it. Small tables were placed almost erratically against what looked like wrought-iron railing. The railing was painted gold; the carpet beneath the table was red. Every few minutes, Culhane made himself blink to clear the red and gold from his vision. Morrison drank Scotch. "Fanny Mulrooney likes Scotch—tastes like medicine to me," Culhane commented.

"At least Scotch is a real drink, not blended whiskey like you're having," Morrison replied.

Culhane sipped at his double shot of Seagrams Seven on the rocks with a splash. It tasted good to him.

"Look at that guy over there, but don't make it obvious," Morrison suggested.

Culhane followed Morrison's cigar-smoke squint to a tall, well-tanned man with a shock of black hair. He wore bush shorts and a khaki shirt with the long sleeves rolled nearly up to the armpits. "He's packing," Morrison said. "I can see it in his eyes. Probably some kind of crotch holster. Maybe that Smith & Wesson pop-up rig. You seen those?"

"Yeah, I've got one back home," Culhane responded. "But I don't see where you say the guy's packing."

"I've got the eye for it, Josh. Saved my bacon more than once, too, let me tell you. You get a tan like that fella's got only one way—playing war in the desert—learned that when I was a foreign correspondent."

"What?" Culhane started to choke on his drink, observing the man again as he wandered the casino floor, apparently just looking at the gaming in progress.

"Some kind of damned terrorist, I'd bet," Morrison said with an air of definitiveness.

"What would a terrorist be doing wandering around here, Ed?"

"Maybe after us, Josh. You think about it. This conference has all the top adventure writers in North America, all under one roof. Who do we send our good guys after?''

Culhane shrugged, setting down his drink. "Terrorists, I know."

"You got it. This guy's probably scouting the place out. Maybe a hit's planned on the conference. I'll tell Thom about it."

"Come on, Ed, be reasonable. Most of these guys at the conference wouldn't be worth the trouble, myself included."

"How did you pick up that limp I noticed?"

Culhane glanced down at his right leg. He hadn't realized he was still limping. "Ah, well, I was down in Latin America doing some research, and—"

"Yeah—that kind of research is going to get you killed someday."

Culhane said nothing.

"As for some of the rest of these guys—hell, they've probably never pulled a trigger on a gray squirrel, let alone something that shot back. But still in all, how many millions of people are swayed against terrorism just by reading the books guys like you and me write?"

"Maybe a lot, I guess." Culhane shrugged. "But why—"

"Probably to silence the voices speaking out against them. You got your heat in that suitcase?"

Culhane looked at the suitcase on the floor beside his feet, then hurriedly around them. Through his teeth, he answered, "Yeah, why?"

"Keep it handy. This might not wind up the bubble-gum-and-sweet-vermouth party it's supposed to be, Josh. Just take a tip from me. What've you got—same hardware Sean Dodge uses in your books?"

Culhane looked behind him, then leaned forward. "Detonics Scoremaster and a Detonics Combat Master. Milt Sparks Six-Pack for the Scoremaster...185-grain Federal JHPs. And my Bali-Song knife."

"Good," Morrison said, nodding.

"Well, I'm glad you're pleased. But I brought the stuff along because I'm meeting Fanny in the desert after the conference is over—another one of her damned-fool wild-goose chases."

"Shit." Morrison laughed. "What's she after now—flying saucers, vampires or zombies?"

Culhane smiled, lit another cigarette and stated, "She's going after the Seven Golden Cities of Cibola. Some old prospector sent a letter to her and claims to have actually been there, wherever the hell 'there' is."

"Seven Golden Cities of Cibola, huh—well, why not? Doesn't sound like something she'll get herself into trouble with, at least," Morrison said as he laughed.

"No, she won't get into trouble," Culhane agreed. "Fanny will wait and get me into trouble. That's what she'll do."

Culhane took a swallow of his drink. Putting the glass on the table, he turned around. The man Morrison had pegged as some sort of desert warrior was still wandering the casino. Culhane studied the man. He couldn't see a gun. Morrison knew his stuff, he thought, but still . . .

Culhane looked away, back at Ed Morrison. Morrison was ordering another round of drinks. "On the house, anyway—why the hell not?"

Culhane didn't know what to say.

8

Only Jess Adolphi had accompanied him in the elevator from the gambling floor to his executive offices on the top floor of the Vegas Crown Hotel. And Jess, the most trusted of his bodyguards, sat now on the opposite side of the office.

Joe Capezi studied Jess Adolphi. Adolphi sat reading a thriller novel—one of a series called The Takers. Capezi had read one once on a cross-country flight, but books held little interest for him. Adolphi, he knew, devoured each new one in the series as it came out.

Capezi remembered his father always saying, "Readers are leaders—like they say, huh, Joe!" and then giving him a friendly slap on the neck. This most recent visit with his father hadn't been terribly friendly. The old man had seemed withdrawn, angry and tormented.

Capezi stood up, checking the time on the gold Rolex President he wore on his left wrist. "Hell, where'd it go?" he murmured.

"Somethin' wrong, Joe?" It was Adolphi.

"Yeah, there's something wrong, Jess. I'm fucking tired—that's what's wrong. Fly out to Miami, sit around with the relatives, go to my sister's funeral, get followed around by the FBI and the local Florida cops, then sit around some more with the relatives. Then talk with my father. The family meeting's still taking place in two weeks, by the way. There's lots of shit wrong— you can bet on that. Hell," and Capezi sat down at his desk again, lighting a cigarette. "Old man and his god-damned meeting. He wants to check out the operation here. 'Something wrong, Joe?'" he mimicked. "Fuck, yes!" He swiveled his chair around and kicked his feet up on the desk.

Joe Capezi looked to his left. Adolphi was already rising. His right hand had dropped the book and was moving under the left side of his sport coat. "Relax, Jess," Capezi said. He hated guns. The only time he had killed he had used a knife—and liked it. But the figure coming through the doorway, customarily not knocking, required neither gun nor knife to deal with. "Milton! It's good to see you. How's the cold?"

Capezi watched as his short, slightly built and balding accountant adjusted his glasses on the bridge of his nose and smiled. "The cold is much better, Mr. Capezi. Thank you for remembering," Milton replied.

"'Thank you for remembering'—what, you sounding like Bob Hope now, Milton?" And Joe Capezi laughed. "Come on, Milton, sit down and tell me what you found out."

Milton glanced at Jess Adolphi, then looked back to Capezi. Capezi smiled. "Jess—hit the trail," he ordered. "And roust Linda from the pool and tell her to get her ass in here in fifteen minutes. Airplane rides always make me horny." Capezi laughed and gestured toward Milton again, saying, "Now—come on, Milton—let's sit down and you tell me all about it, huh?"

Milton nodded and marched toward the desk in short, shuffling strides. Under his left arm a file folder bulged with yellow sheets of paper. He stood for a moment, then sat down in the straight-backed chair opposite Joe Capezi.

Capezi swung his feet down, stood and walked toward the wall of sliding glass doors leading out onto his patio. Sun streamed through the sheers. He studied the penthouse pool, the one the guests never used, never saw. He could see Jess Adolphi approaching the lounge chair draped with beach towels and the figure of the tanned, blond girl resting there—Linda. "So tell me the bad news, Milton. Sure as hell can't be good news," he said as he turned back into the room and studied Milton's face. "Can't be good news the way you're looking."

Milton cleared his throat. "I'm afraid you're right, Mr. Capezi. It isn't good news."

"Give it to me fast—Linda will be coming." He considered the double meaning in his words.

Milton cleared his throat again. "Mr. Capezi—senior, that is—has tapped into our computer system. His computer operators have read the entries made in our private program, and by now I'm sure they've decoded them sufficiently to realize it is a bookkeeping system. Oh, I almost forgot. Please forgive me. My sorrow on the death of—"

"The hell with my sister—she was always a goody-goody pain in the ass, anyway. Get on with what you were saying, Milton," and Joe Capezi turned back to the window and watched as Linda uncoiled from her lounge chair and stretched. He looked at her long legs and thought about how she wrapped them around him when they made love. Milton's voice brought him back. "In another few days they will have had ample opportunity to penetrate the entire system, to learn the entire program and therefore break the code for our secret bookkeeping system. Then your father will know everything. He'll know about the twelve million dollars you've skimmed in the past six years and—"

"Why don't we pull the plug on the machine?" Capezi asked, still staring out of the window.

"You asked me that when I first alerted you to the problem, Mr. Capezi. They'd know for certain then that we had something to hide. I've run all the down time I can risk without them realizing we're trying to block them. And as you said yourself, Mr. Capezi, if your father thinks you're trying to hide something, he'll send his own people out here and—"

"What if the whole system were gone—I mean, permanently gone?" Capezi wondered aloud. Linda was less than ten yards from the doors—he'd have her in a minute.

"Then the records would be irretrievable, Mr. Capezi. But, ah, computers don't just lose records or get accidentally erased. And the entire system could only be destroyed if the entire twenty-third floor were destroyed, as we have discussed, and—"

Capezi turned to Milton. "Get out of here, Milton. I got bones to jump. Keep the computer running some kind of program until we can solve this. Make certain that no information can be retrieved at all."

"I've been doing that, Mr. Capezi, but—"

"Never mind the 'but'—huh? Be a good boy, Milton—do as you're told. Now get out but stay around. Sleep in the hotel tonight. Have Adolphi fix it so you get a nice room, maybe a girl if you want one."

"Mr. Capezi—I mean—"

"Get out," and he dismissed Milton from his mind and turned to watch Linda.

9

It was a habit he'd picked up from Fanny Mulrooney. At some time or another, in every hotel where they had ever stayed together, she would open each dresser drawer, each nightstand drawer.

He sat on the edge of the bed on the balcony side and opened the nightstand drawer.

Culhane laughed. "Charles Dickens must've been thinking about this place when he wrote *Great Expectations*," he whispered to himself. Inside the drawer were a dozen individually packaged prophylactics.

He closed the drawer. Assuming that was the man's side of the king-size bed, he rolled across to the other side and opened the other nightstand.

A Gideon Bible.

He wondered if that was to give the girl something to do while— "Naw," he said, shaking his head.

Culhane looked at his watch, suddenly remembering the wake-up call. It was six-fifteen. Dinner was at seven. Naked, he stood up, stretched. He exhaled hard and walked into the bathroom to urinate. . . .

HIS CALISTHENICS DONE, then a brief tae kwon-do *cata*, Culhane brushed his teeth, debating while he did so whether he needed a second shave that day. It was six thirty-five—which meant it was really nine thirty-five in terms of the shave. Grudgingly he nodded at his face in the mirror as he worked the waxed dental floss between his teeth. Finished with the dental floss, he opened the black box for his old Norelco, found the electrical outlet and plugged it in. He checked that the setting hadn't shifted off number six and flicked the razor on. As he shaved, he studied his face. The way he traveled between books, researching in the field, he almost invariably had a good tan. His brown eyes were clear, despite the confusing sleep schedule. In the fluorescent light of the bathroom mirror, he could see no gray in his brown hair, but there seemed to be plenty of red in it. He shut off the razor, rubbing his hands over his face below his sideburns, across his chin, his upper lip. Smooth. Perhaps not the best shave he'd ever had, but satisfactory. He unplugged the razor, replaced it in the case and glanced at his watch again. The shower would have to be fast....

CULHANE WORE CHARCOAL-GRAY SLACKS, a medium-blue, long-sleeved shirt—he rarely bothered with short-sleeved shirts because long sleeves could always be rolled up and a short sleeve was restricted to just that—and a blue silk knit tie. He owned three ties, all silk knit, all made in Italy, all purchased from Neiman Marcus—one blue, one brown, one black. He stepped into his black Florsheims as he threaded his belt through the loops. Perhaps it had been the influence of Ed Morrison and all his talk about terrorists, but he threaded on a holster he'd been trying out for the little Detonics .45, one from Thad Rybka that rode at a radical angle in the small of the back. The holster in place, he reached to the night-table top—the one with the rubbers in the drawer—and picked up the Detonics Combat Master stainless, working the slide. Despite the fact that cocked and locked was a faster-into-action carrying mode and safer to the wearer, he did as he almost invariably did unless expecting instant trouble. He lowered the hammer over the chambered round, rolling his left thumb between the hammer and the frame as an added precaution. He holstered the little .45, then walked across the room and slipped on his blue Cricketeer blazer.

He left the button open to better hide the gun, then glanced at himself once in the full-length mirror in the bathroom door—the gun didn't show when he bent over.

Culhane grabbed his keys, his wallet, his money clip, two packs of cigarettes, his handkerchief and his lighter. He doubted he'd encounter too many blood-crazed terrorists—he smiled at the thought—and decided not to bother with a spare magazine for the Detonics.

Culhane let himself out. . . .

FATE HAD WILLED IT, Culhane decided. As he stepped out of one of the elevators that opened onto the main floor, Ed Morrison—rumpled dark-blue suit, white shirt and indifferently striped tie at half-mast—stepped from another. "Hey, Josh—going to the big bash?"

"Yeah—I think I'm even awake."

As Morrison fell in beside him, Culhane felt the man's hand tap gently at the small of his back. "Good carry, Josh," Morrison praised him under his breath. "None of Capezi's goons will spot it there," and he moved his hand away. "Old hooker's trick," he explained, "to see if a prospective john is the law, instead. Start between the shoulder blades and feel for the shoulder harness. I just started lower on you—that coat wouldn't take a shoulder rig," and Morrison lit one of his cigars.

Culhane just shook his head, striking up a Pall Mall and knifing through the crowd beside Morrison.

As they started for the doors leading to the outside world, Morrison jabbed Culhane's left side with his elbow. Culhane looked at him, then past him. It was the desert warrior again, changed from his shorts and military shirt to a khaki-colored suit with no tie. The white shirt in combination with his dark hair made the deepness of his tan all that much more noticeable. "Probably a pimp for one of the girl ranches," Culhane suggested.

"Nope—got a gun again, too," Morrison said. "Strong side carry—see the way the coat breaks at his right kidney?"

Culhane couldn't see it. He asked the obvious question of Morrison, "Are you carrying?"

"I almost never do anymore, Josh. Leave that to you younger fellas."

They went through the first bank of glass doors—the air conditioning was colder there, or at least seemed that way—then through the second set into the neon-and-glitter night. The air felt thick, humid, almost something you could taste, Culhane thought, making a mental note to remember the impression in case he ever set a book in Las Vegas. As they walked down the hotel driveway to the street—the dinner meeting was at the hotel across the street—Culhane noticed a scruffy-looking teenager, his left arm loaded with small tabloid-sized newspapers. The kid shoved one at him, and Culhane glanced at it as they waited for the light at the crowded corner; in the canyon of neon surrounding them, it was bright enough to read. Culhane took his glasses from his breast pocket, settling the wire frames on his head. The newspaper advertised girls and their services. "Aw, shit," Culhane snarled, stuffing the paper into a trash can as they started across the street with the crowd.

Morrison was laughing. He glanced over at Culhane, then said, "Me, I'm lucky—I'll be dead by then. But you, well, welcome to the twenty-first century—" and Ed Morrison gestured expansively around them.

Overweight people in beach clothes pushed and jostled—to get where? Culhane wondered. He adjusted his glasses, looked at Ed Morrison and said, "Want to trade prognoses?"

All Morrison did was laugh.

10

As he worked the handle on the slot, Mordecai Nitsch noticed two things: the old woman standing beside him at the machine stank of urine and wore a glove on her right hand as she worked the lever, and the men he had seen earlier were at it again, collecting money from the banks at the various tables filling the casino floor. He checked his watch. It was precisely 7:00 P.M.

Mordecai Nitsch made no point of staring at the men, for he knew he in turn was being watched—mirrors formed a wide molding between the walls and ceiling of the entire casino floor at the Vegas Crown, and he knew they were two-way mirrors. Occasionally, when there was a lapse in the din, he could just barely make out the buzz of a security camera moving to scan something one of the watchers found interesting.

A uniformed security officer walked past him, and Mordecai Nitsch dipped into the pockets of his tan suit to find another coin for the slot. The security officers were by and large former big-city police officers, experienced men. He knew their weapons. The choice of service revolvers was theirs, whether .38 Special or .357 Magnum Colt or Smith & Wesson or Ruger or Dan Wesson. But choice of ammo was not; they were limited to the 158-grain .38 Special SPD Load, the lead hollowpoint. A good expander plus P.

Mordecai Nitsch liked other things better, like the 9mm Beretta 92SB in the holster against his right kidney or the Glaser safety slugs in the blue Chiefs Special on his left ankle. He had taken the Chiefs, its holster and the restricted Glaser from a police officer he had killed in Ohio.

He worked the slot, not winning.

He plastered a smile on his face and walked away, gravitating toward the small lounge on the mezzanine at the rear of the casino floor. A scantily clad girl walked past him, selling Keno, and he shook his head to indicate he wasn't interested in playing.

Nitsch stopped at the third step leading up to the lounge and surveyed the casino floor behind him. This time the smile that crossed his lips was spontaneous.

He walked to the bar, sitting down on a vacant stool beside a woman in a black cocktail dress, diamonds dripping from her neck and earlobes. She was past middle age, but pretty enough, he supposed.

He told the bartender, "A double Jack Daniels Black Label, straight up," and he glanced again at the woman. Their eyes met. Her glass was empty. "And the lady will have another—"

"Vodka martini," she supplied. "With Smirnoff 100."

He nodded at the bartender and turned to look more intently at the woman.

THOM HARK STOOD UP at the head of the table, an embarrassed smile on his face as he bent slightly forward. "Gentlemen, please—why don't we argue tomorrow at the actual meeting. Gentlemen?"

Culhane watched and smiled. He turned his eyes from the wiry, sandy-brown-haired, bespectacled Englishman who was his editor, to the far end of the table, where Ed Morrison was busily and heatedly arguing with one of the other authors.

"Ed?" It was Hark again, his Ronald Colemanesque voice tinged with urgency.

Morrison looked away from his adversary and across the table at Hark. "What is it, Thom?"

"I was just wondering if you might not enjoy arguing more tomorrow than this evening. This is a social gathering, but we do have one or two points we wish to touch on."

"Okay, Thom—you touch on your one or two points, and then I'll go back to arguing. Fair enough?"

Hark laughed out loud. "Fair enough, then."

Culhane leaned back in his chair, lighting a Pall Mall. He liked Ed Morrison a great deal. It was Ed who had originally got him out of writing magazine articles and into writing books. And he liked Thom Hark—a fair man with a good sense of humor. He knew that Hark and Ed Morrison got along, as well.

Culhane glanced at Bob Meadowshed, seated beside him. Meadowshed's face was expressionless beneath the strands of blond hair that crossed his forehead and the mustache that covered his upper lip. Meadowshed winked. Culhane looked away, back toward Hark.

"As I indicated to Ed," Hark began, "this is not a formal meeting. But some business can be accomplished between drinks, and I promise—" and Hark smiled "—that the business will be short." There was a round of applause, and Hark bowed slightly, laughing. "Thank you very much. Well, I am to formally instruct all of you that—" he paused with dramatic flair "—you are all fired." There wasn't a reaction. "Bad joke, I suppose." And his voice built in intensity. "Actually, just the opposite, really. Everyone is so happy with the books that we should be paying you more money than we do. But we won't do that, at least not for the moment." There was a chorus of boos and hisses. "Thank you again. But in all seriousness, the books by and large are superb—a few rough edges, a few ever-so-slightly-missed deadlines, but no serious complaints." Culhane thought Hark had glanced at him with the remark about missed deadlines. "We'll get into all the specifics tomorrow, of course, but I want us all to consider a few possibilities. Art mirrors life, and sometimes unfortunately life mirrors art. There is a common thread running through the adventure series that all of you are aware of—terrorism. To a man, I'd say, each of you first elected to have terrorist villains for your heroes to fight because of the global terrorist problem. But recently, in reality, the terrorist problem has become considerably more serious, and I'm inclined to believe that your books should reflect this new terrorist wave. Let's all think quite seriously regarding new ways in which the counterterrorists about which nearly all of you write can employ their talents against the fictional counterparts of heightened terrorist activity in the real world. Does that make any sense?''

Bob Meadowshed spoke. ''You want us to pull out all the stops, the way terrorists are doing it for real.''

''Exactly. Unfortunately for the real world, terrorists seem possessed of nearly unbridled imaginative skills. And we must, too.''

''What happens,'' Ed asked, ''if we accidentally start giving the terrs ideas? They start getting their plots from us?''

''Can I try to answer that?'' Culhane interjected.

''Please.'' Thom Hark nodded.

''When you touch on something really sensitive, use a form of self-imposed censorship. I've got contacts I'd be willing to share with any of you. From time to time, simply run a story past the right people. I don't really change anything, but if I accidentally have one of my bad guys find a chink in the armor of the real-life good guy, then the real-life good guy knows about it in advance of the book's hitting the stands and can fix the hole in his scenario. And it's a two-way street. When I hear about new gadgets and techniques from somebody who actually does the stuff we just write about, there's never any worry I'm going to blow something sensitive. It works quite well for me,'' Culhane concluded.

"Where's the dessert?" Bob Meadowshed asked.

"Yeah, how about a cake with a girl coming out of it?" Morrison piped in.

Culhane looked at his fellow adventure writers, then at Thom Hark. "I give up," he said.

"Yes, tomorrow we must try to be a little less serious," Hark said.

11

Mordecai Nitsch turned the wheel of the Ford Mustang, double-clutching as he downshifted into second for the tight turn onto the dirt road. There had been an uncharacteristic light rain, and he was having problems getting traction as he moved the white car along the ranch road, constantly upshifting and downshifting between second and third. The high beams danced crazily in front of him.

Nitsch turned up the narrow gravel driveway leading to the ranch itself. He dropped into first, letting engine compression all but stop the Mustang, barely touching the brakes.

He'd cut the lights as he'd turned up the driveway, and now he turned the key—the Mustang coughed once and then went silent. He wrenched the emergency brake up, then opened the door and stepped out, pocketing the Ford's keys.

He heard a woman's voice. "Mordecai?"

"No—it is the FBI, Charlene—you had better shoot."

He walked toward the house. The lights were going on; the door was already cracked open, and now a beam of yellow light from inside speared the darkness, making the darkness deeper, the shadow greater.

He mounted the three low steps and walked inside.

Charlene—as tanned as he was but her tan somehow looking better than a suntan ever did on a man—threw her long, strong arms around his neck and embraced him. He smelled her perfume—Chanel No. 5, one of the few fragrances he could always identify.

He pushed her back and her black eyes momentarily showed the rebuff. Then a smile crinkled the corners of her wide mouth. "We were beginning to worry, Mord— I was beginning to worry."

He touched his right hand to her left cheek, running his fingers along the smoothness of her skin and into her shoulder-length, dark-brown curls. "I'm fine. All went well with the operation, too," and he moved his hand away and walked past her toward the kitchen. He could hear Charlene's bare feet padding along the threadbare carpet runner behind him.

The kitchen was exceedingly large—and it was good that it was, Nitsch thought. Five dozen men filled it, standing beside the counters, seated at the long refectory table, perched on wooden stools. The center of the table was cluttered with Uzi submachine guns and spare magazines for them, ashtrays brimming over with cigarette butts and half-crushed cans of American beer. The beer smell pervaded the kitchen. Clouds of gray cigarette smoke formed ten feet above the floor by the double banks of fluorescent lights.

Charlene was the only woman, and when she entered the room, one of the men—Moishe Sebin—made to give her his stool beside the stove. She smiled, shaking her head, and leaned against the counter top beside him, instead. Sebin lit a cigarette and handed it to her. Nitsch watched as her cheeks hollowed when she inhaled the smoke. He noticed the pale lipstick marks on the white cigarette paper as she passed the cigarette back to Sebin. She was trying to make him jealous, Nitsch realized. He also realized it was working. Sebin was five years younger and an inch taller—a blond-haired Jewish Adonis.

Mentally Nitsch said, "Who gives a fuck," then laughed at the subconscious double entendre. Apparently Charlene gave such a commodity.

"You are late," Sebin announced.

"You're very observant, Moishe—I am late."

"We have all been waiting," Sebin responded.

"I can see that from the cigarette smoke in the air and smell it from the beer. Finish what you have," he said, cracking the command whip, walking deeper into the room to stand beside Charlene. "But there will be no more drinking. We go as planned. History will be made—this may be the largest robbery in the history of all casino robberies anywhere."

"And the bloodiest," Charlene noted, smiling up at him.

He dismissed the remark. "We have found that kidnappings bring only modest returns. But the return from this enterprise shall be great, indeed." He looked at Sebin. "You have checked your explosives?"

"Obviously. When we leave the hotel, we activate our detonators and the hotel is—" and Sebin's long, slender fingers made an upward, explosive gesture toward the ceiling "—whoosh!"

"That Mafia bastard who went after our men in Miami—" Charlene began.

"Don Carlo Capezi," one of the others supplied, dry-spitting into the air.

"Capezi will learn that the tragedy he experienced in Florida will be nothing compared to the penalty he shall suffer with the destruction of his entire empire of sin," another of the men added.

Mordecai Nitsch found himself laughing. "'His empire of sin'? His casino and his hotel will be rubble. Hundreds, perhaps thousands of his guests and patrons and employees will be killed or maimed. And we talk of his sin?" He lit a cigarette. Some of the others were laughing with him now.

Nitsch raised his left wrist and studied the face of his watch. "You will begin to infiltrate the hotel in three hours and eight minutes from now—let's synchronize our watches. The assault will begin at precisely 9 A.M. You know the signal, and each of you has rehearsed your part. Our revenge against Don Carlo Capezi is merely icing on the cake, as our American hosts say. What we want is the money, and the total destruction of the Vegas Crown to cover our withdrawal. Keep this in mind—we are soldiers...this is a military operation. We are avengers only secondarily.''

There were nods and the flickerings of eyes as all the faces in the kitchen in the desert ranch house registered their commitment.

Nitsch walked across the kitchen diagonally, opening one of the cupboards above the refrigerator. His own Mini-Uzi was stored there, and he took it down, along with the nylon GI fanny pack that held the spare magazines. He shoved the pack under his arm, checked the Uzi's bolt function, then inserted the one loose magazine.

"And remember," he said as he smiled and turned to his force. "Some of you especially. The casinos don't welcome vagrants—so get the beer off your breath." As he started from the kitchen, he looked at his watch again and added, "I will see you at the Vegas Crown in three hours and six minutes."

He walked through the band of darkness at the center of the hallway, stopping as he heard the sound of Charlene's bare feet on the carpet runner again.

He turned to face her.

"Mordecai," she whispered, "with Moishe back there—it was only to—"

"To make me jealous," he concluded for her.

"Yes. I love you so," she said, her lips pouting, "but you seem not to notice me sometimes. But then other times—"

His right hand found the small of her back, drawing her close against him in the shadow. His Uzi swung on its sling at his right side.

He could see her face, half in shadow, half in light. He kissed the parted lips, feeling the moist warmth of her mouth, feeling her heart pounding and her breasts beneath the fabric of the khaki shirt she wore—opened half to her waist—hot against him.

"I have a lot on my mind," he whispered in her left ear, kissing the lobe gently. "After this is through—it will be just the two of us, Charlene."

She stepped back from him and he watched her tongue moisten her lips, making the skin glisten in the fragmentary light. "Just the two of us," she murmured like a litany.

Nitsch turned and walked toward the hall door, through the wash of yellow light and into the moonlit darkness.

He opened the rear deck of the Mustang, placing the Uzi under a deflated air mattress and the fanny pack of spare magazines beside it. He closed the deck and looked back into the house, still tasting Charlene in his mouth.

THIS ROAD WAS A MUCH BETTER ONE, well paved, and with the moonlight he barely needed even his low beams as he slowed the Mustang before the rustic, wooden, corral-fence gate. A man in a cowboy hat, designer jeans and plaid cowboy shirt walked to the fence as the gate opened inward automatically. He waved toward the Mustang, and Nitsch noticed the revolver on the man's right hip—a little snubby .38 Special in a holster that would be too slow to do any good if the man ever really needed it.

"Yes, sir—good evening," the cowboy greeted him.

"Good evening," Nitsch said through his open window. "I read your ad. I'm a stranger in town and—"

The cowboy grinned. "Everybody's a stranger here, partner. You don't have any drugs or firearms on you, do you?"

"Of course not," Nitsch answered.

"Drive on in, then. Park on the left side of the building—follow the arrows. And have a good time. Don't forget to lock your car now."

Nitsch nodded. "Thank you. Thank you very much."

He stepped on the gas and drove through.

He had watched the American television series "Bonanza" on occasion, and he thought, as he approached the ranch house in the moonlight, following the arrows, turning into the parking lot and finding a vacant slot, that it looked like a larger-than-life version of the Ponderosa spread.

He stopped the Mustang, killed the engine, rolled up his driver's-side window and climbed out, locking the Mustang as he'd been told.

He started across the well-lit parking lot, staring up at the nearly full moon. Its brightness obscured the stars except at the very edge of the circular horizon line. He climbed the steps to the front porch. He supposed the thing to do was to knock. So he did.

The door opened, and a pleasant-looking man in a cowboy-style suit stood in front of him. He looked Nitsch up and down.

Nitsch cleared his throat. He had never had the occasion to use the services of a whorehouse before—he had always got what he wanted free, or at best the cost of a dinner or a bottle of wine or both.

"I, ah, I read the ad and—"

"Come on in. Make yourself comfortable in the parlor there, and we'll have somebody right out to help you." The well-dressed cowboy smiled. "My name's Willie."

"My name is Morde—"

"Mort's just fine." The man nodded, closing the door behind Nitsch as he stepped through, then gesturing toward the room off to Nitsch's left.

Nitsch said nothing as he walked into the room and sat down on a leather-looking vinyl sofa. He picked up a copy of a girlie magazine and leafed through it.

He heard footsteps—his hearing was exceptionally good and had saved his life in combat on innumerable occasions—but he didn't look up. He was a man visiting a whorehouse; he wasn't supposed to be using his combat senses.

"Mort? Willie said you was Mort."

Now he looked up; a pretty middle-aged woman with a plastic smile was bending toward him. "Yes—I was, ah—" Nitsch stammered.

"We take all major credit cards," the woman said, still smiling. "But I'm afraid we don't take personal checks unless they're drawn on a local bank."

"I—I have credit cards," Nitsch supplied.

"Good. Well, what would you like?"

He wondered if he should make up something strange, but instead he said, "I'm looking for a lay, that's all." That wasn't entirely the truth, but there was no reason for the madam to know it....

IN THE BACK PARLOR he met the available girls—there was something for everyone, he had to admit to himself. He had no trouble making a decision. The blond, blue-eyed girl who looked like some sweet thing fresh off a kibbutz had been his choice, and he had let her lead him by the hand out of the parlor, down the small corridor and up the winding, rough-cut log staircase onto the second floor, then down another corridor to the last room on the left.

The girl used a small latchkey, opened the door and stepped inside. "Anything special? I mean—" the girl began.

"Do I want you to wear boots, or something? Something like that?" Nitsch said.

"Yeah—it doesn't cost extra."

"Thank you very much," Nitsch said politely. "But I thought maybe we could just undress and get into bed."

"Suit yourself," she replied, forcing a smile. "Do you want to undress me?"

"All right—I'd like that," and he realized that he really did want to. She turned her back to him and he raised her hair, finding the zipper at the back of her dress. It was a larger than usual zipper, and he wondered if it was industrial sized, made to take a lot of use. He worked it down to just above the crack in her behind—she wore no bra, no panties. He leaned over and kissed her shoulder blades, left then right. She hunched her shoulders and the dress fell forward, from her arms to her waist. Her body twitched almost imperceptibly and the dress fell to the floor around her feet.

Naked, she turned to him. "I'll undress you now."

Nitsch said nothing and watched as she opened his shirt at the center button midway down his chest. Her hands drifted under the shirt—he could feel her fingers prod at his nipples and it made him feel goose bumps on the backs of his arms and the fronts of his thighs. He felt her hands moving, undressing him, felt them stop as they found the Beretta automatic under his coat. The hands moved on as her voice whispered into his right ear, "You had better remove that yourself—put it on the nightstand if you like."

He left her then, removing both pistols and the black Gerber MkI fighting knife. He set all three arms on the nightstand. He returned to her, and she continued undressing him, kneeling in front of him as she removed his pants. Her lips brushed against him. "That's a little something extra, for a little something extra," she told him. He didn't answer. She continued undressing him; she took his hand and they walked the few steps to the bed. She stepped out of her high heels and sat down, her small breasts, thrusting slightly upward, cupped momentarily above her palms. She leaned back, her thighs spread slightly apart.

Nitsch sat down on the edge of the bed, after a moment feeling her hands against his back.

She rolled back as he looked at her, and he turned to rest beside her, feeling her hands on him, exploring her body with his hands. As he rolled on top of her, he could feel her hands guiding him inside her, feel her breath against his cheek.

She whispered, "I couldn't help but notice—are you Jewish?"

"My parents had me circumcised as a whim." He laughed, feeling the friction, then the wetness. He studied her face for a moment. "Your lips—they are like the touch of a hummingbird's wing." He felt slightly ridiculous saying it.

"I feel strength in you," she responded.

He continued to look at her. "For a moment, I was wondering—"

"This is like any other cover, Mordecai Nitsch—to be believable, it must be perfected. Make love to me while we talk—if you like."

"Yes, Hummingbird, I would like that," and he bent his head to kiss the nipples of her breasts.

Her voice low, her breath against him, he heard her say, "The controller has prepared what you need."

"Potempkin?" he asked.

"Yes, Potempkin, but you are not to use that name, even though it is only the controller's code name. You are not to use it."

"The papers will be clear?"

"As clear as they can be. We have used one of the Mossad codes they do not yet know we have broken. But the Americans have it or can get it. The papers will be read."

"I do not think that documents such as these will be sufficient."

"There are persons whom we can trust who will make much of an Israeli commando team under orders of the Mossad destroying a Las Vegas hotel. We have linked Don Carlo Capezi—" she cooed in his left ear, then bit it "—to arms being smuggled into Libya, terrorist arms turned against Israel."

"This is such an obvious lie. I think the Americans will suspect—"

"During the Second World War, Capezi was a consultant to the OSS for the invasion of Sicily. He kept contacts with the CIA throughout the years. We have improved upon this. It will appear that he became disaffected with the CIA and engaged in the arms smuggling to Libya by way of getting back at his former friends. The documents are quite specific, but not so specific as to appear obviously spurious. It is the perfect motive for Israeli revenge. Trust the documents—they were well prepared," and she added after biting his left earlobe again, "I am told. What you need is zipped into the seat cushion of the chair where I placed your jacket. You can take the documents anytime you wish."

"What about the operation in Miami? Will the men who—"

"Steps are being taken to neutralize the possibility after the interference. Now you can go," she teased.

He hesitated, feeling something welling inside of him.

"Or you can stay a little longer, if you like—if it pleases your body or your soul or both," she whispered.

She leaned her head back then. He looked at her for an instant. "Hummingbird—a lovely name."

The corners of her mouth upturned in what he thought might be a smile.

He looked away from the smile to work over the body with his own. He was trembling.

But she no longer bit at him or touched him with her lips. Yet neither did she interfere with the pleasure he took.

12

Bob Meadowshed had bought the current round of drinks. Culhane leaned back, lighting a cigarette, watching Meadowshed absently, watching the casino floor from the mezzanine bar with morbid fascination. He had been to Vegas before, and he had been other places where gambling was a way of life. But the idea of people paying for the privilege of losing money they had worked hard to earn never ceased to amaze him.

Meadowshed tapped him on the arm. "What do you think, Josh?"

Culhane shook his head and turned to Meadowshed, smiling, "I lost you," he said. "Back up a little—I'm sorry."

"No, that's all right. What I was saying was this—" and he looked around the table, taking a cigarette from his case, lighting it "—take you, or take Ed here."

"Nobody'd take me—hell." Morrison laughed, sipping at his Scotch.

"Or take me," Meadowshed continued. "The three of us have all done some of the stuff we have our guys do."

"Yeah, but we never met all the dames the guys in the books do," and Morrison laughed.

Culhane suddenly thought of Fanny Mulrooney and her old prospector. He wondered if she was any closer to the Seven Golden Cities of Cibola. "Sometimes we do," he said.

It was the fourth man at the table, Aaron Flaherty—the newest addition to the growing ranks of adventure writers under the aegis of their common publisher—who laughed, saying, "I understand you and that crazy-assed broad M.F. Mulrooney are living together. What kind of house you got—Dracula's coffin or a UFO?"

Meadowshed groaned, muttered, "Oh, boy," and looked away.

Ed Morrison quietly picked up his drink, almost whispering, "Mr. Flaherty, you're the stupidest son of a bitch I have recently had the misfortune of meeting."

Culhane watched Flaherty's eyes as Flaherty turned away from Morrison. "Aaron—may I call you 'Aaron'?" Culhane said. He didn't wait for an answer. "You ever mention Mary Frances Mulrooney's name in front of me again, or to anybody else ever again, and I'll rip your fucking tongue out and then ram it up your ass with my foot."

Culhane didn't move his eyes from Flaherty as he stood up. Then he turned toward Bob Meadowshed. "Bob, thanks for the drink. See you tomorrow." He looked at Ed Morrison. Morrison was grinning like the Cheshire cat in *Alice in Wonderland*. "Ed—breakfast?"

"Yeah—I haven't tried that for a few years. What the hell, I'll call your room and set the time."

"Right." Culhane nodded and looked at Aaron Flaherty. "Aaron, I hope you sleep restlessly and have a wet dream."

Culhane picked up his cigarettes and lighter, pocketed them and walked down the three steps onto the casino floor.

He started for the elevator banks, looking down the long cordon sanitaire between the elevators and the casino floor. Coming through the doors was the desert warrior, his khaki suit looking a little more rumpled than before, bony fingers combing back his hair.

The desert warrior was walking toward the elevators. Culhane looked to the doors in front of him. None was opening.

The khaki-clad figure stood beside him. The racket of the casino and a band starting up somewhere consumed the background. The desert warrior leaned forward, punching the elevator call button with the middle finger of his right hand. As he moved, Culhane thought he caught the fabric of the man's suit coat breaking over something beside the right kidney.

Culhane looked away, back toward the bar, saying half aloud, "Ed?"

The desert warrior, his voice slightly accented, asked, "Did you say something to me?"

Culhane looked at him. There was a dinging sound, and Culhane glanced at the elevator bank. One of the elevators, obviously not the one he stood in front of, was opening. "No—no—just thinking out loud."

The desert warrior started for the elevator, saying nothing. Culhane followed him. His curiosity was piqued, and he wondered if he should follow the man to his floor. Just in case.

Culhane shook his head and thought, Jeez, Ed—now you've got me doing it, and started for the elevator.

He stepped inside as the doors closed, just missing him. The button was already pushed for the eighth floor. Culhane hesitated a moment, then pushed for eight, as well. "My floor, too," he said, and he tried to remember something to whistle.

13

Dan Track moved a half step back from the red Everlast bag Sir Abner had provided for him. The knuckles of his fists hurt in the striking gloves. He pivoted on his bare right foot, swinging onto his left, then delivered a roundhouse kick to the bag with his right. He followed this with a full three-hundred-sixty-degree spin, and launched a high double kick at the top of the bag with the ball of his left foot. He wheeled again, going into a low guard stance, taking a half step forward, punching with the middle knuckles of first his left, then his right hand into the midsection of the bag.

He heard George Beegh's voice behind him on the veranda. "You've got a funny way of relaxing, Uncle Dan."

Stepping back from the bag, Track sucked in his breath, then turned to face George. "It's better with a live sparring partner, son."

George, still wet from his shower, stepped back, grinning, moving his hands like a magician during an epileptic seizure, laughing, saying, "What you call me, fool?"

Track edged left; George moved right, and Track feigned a punch with his left hand to George's face that George half blocked, half sidestepped. Track pivoted on his right foot, tapping the bare toes of his left against George's rib cage on the right, spinning. George swung as Track sidestepped, backed into his nephew and jabbed George in the solar plexus with his left elbow.

His right hand caught George's right forearm, while the left hand grabbed the wrist. Track levered the arm up, then levered it down over his left shoulder at the elbow. His left heel impacted lightly against George's left shin, then snapped out as his left foot back-kicked to George's crotch.

"All right, already—enough!" George protested.

"Like I said, much better with a practice dummy than a bag." Track let go of his nephew's wrist and ran about six steps away.

"Ooh—you're asking for it," George muttered.

"Hell with ya." Track laughed. "I'm going to have some breakfast. Want some?"

"Yeah, thanks."

" 'Thanks' my rear end. Fix it yourself," and Track started for the house, with George running after him.

Track reached the glass door for the veranda, opened and closed the panel and walked across the living room, hearing the door open on its runner behind him, then close again.

Track turned around, smiling. "Not so bad for somebody almost old enough to be your father, huh?"

"Eleven years isn't old enough to be my father—just old enough to be a pain in the butt!" And George was smiling now, too.

Track moved across the room, entering the narrow hall that led to the rear of the house and the kitchen.

He opened the refrigerator, finding the orange juice, then took down a glass from the cupboard. George came into the kitchen. "Want some orange juice?" Track asked.

"Should I?" George replied.

"Yeah," and Track took down another glass, filling both. At the near end of the counter was the half-filled bottle with his One-A-Days. He twisted open the childproof cap and popped one, washing it down with more of the juice. "Why don't you put some water on for coffee while I take a shower?"

"I don't want any coffee."

"I do."

"Then damn well fix it yourself!"

"Okay," and Track took back the untouched glass of orange juice.

"All right, I'll boil some water." His nephew laughed, taking the orange juice and belting it down.

Track poured himself a second glass as George asked, "What time do you leave for Europe and Desiree?"

"Emotionally, that's the wrong order—it's Desiree and Europe—but my flight leaves at three this afternoon. What time do you leave for New Mexico?"

"Just after four—I've got it written down."

Track nodded. "Well, we can head out to the airport together. What are you going to do while I'm gone?"

"Catch up on my reading, my sleeping, my eating—and see what the local population of unattached women is like in a line between Albuquerque and Santa Fe," George said as he fired up a cigarette.

"Sounds like you'll wind up light on the sleep department. Why don't you try quitting cigarettes?"

"When I want to quit, I'll quit," George replied as his head was enveloped in smoke.

"Yeah, tell me about it."

Track walked away, hearing the sounds of water running as George filled the whistling teapot they used to make instant coffee.

He headed into the bathroom, stripping away his clothes, and turned on the water for the shower. He stepped into the shower, still thinking about Desiree Goth, about lying beside her in bed, about things as everyday as just talking to her without an ocean between them.

He stuck his head into the water and yelled, "George! You ran out all the damn hot water! George!"

From the kitchen he could hear his nephew laughing.

FANNY MULROONEY LOOKED at the sign through the windshield wipers and the torrents of rain and read, Los Dos Hermanos, and then beneath that in English, Restaurant. She could believe the Spanish part, but she couldn't quite accept the word "Restaurant." She'd seen more sanitary-looking facilities in public washrooms in the Middle East. But this was Arizona.

She grimaced, shut off the windshield wipers and turned the key, pulling it from the ignition and dropping it into the massive maroon leather shoulder bag on the seat beside her. She began shuffling through the bag. She found her speedloader, but she couldn't find her gun. She kept rummaging. Finding her cigarettes, she took one out and lit it with a Bic lighter. Delving back into the bag, she pushed aside canisters of undeveloped rolls of film, her hairbrush, and a lipstick she'd thought she'd lost. She opened the old lipstick, cranked it up and turned the rearview mirror so she could see her lips. It didn't taste bad. To her, taste was more important than color, but it didn't look bad, either. She put the old lipstick back in her purse, wondering if she'd ever see it again. Then she found her gun. She looked around the parking lot. There were several cars parked in front of the "Two Brothers" restaurant, but no one was standing around in the downpour. She took the little stainless Model 60 S&W from her purse and opened the cylinder. It was loaded. She closed the cylinder, leaving the revolver at the top of her purse, just in case.

Reaching around into the back seat, Mulrooney yanked at the yellow rubber rain jacket, pulled it into the front seat and twisted around from behind the wheel

so she could pull it on. She pulled up the hood, pushing
her shoulder-length auburn hair back under the hood's
protection.

Shouldering her bag, she muttered, "Here goes nothing," and stepped out of the car. The rain was falling in
sheets as she hesitated at the car door and reached into
the back seat again—she'd forgotten her camera bag.
Her white track shoes were already soaked, and her bare
feet felt squishy inside them. She slammed the door
closed on the rental car and went into a dead run across
the parking lot, tugging up the bottoms of her jeans to
keep them out of the puddles.

She reached the cover of the awning over the front of
the restaurant and caught her breath, letting down the
hood of the rain jacket, hearing the tattoo the rain beat
on the metal awning. She shook her hair and started for
the door.

As her hand touched the knob, she sensed a figure approach from her right side and she froze. "You M.F.
Mulrooney?" a gruff voice demanded.

She whirled and a man with a dark-gray, sodden-
looking, broad-brimmed cowboy hat—bigger than the
one Josh Culhane occasionally wore—stepped out from
beside the door. In the yellow light from the restaurant
windows she could barely make out his eyes, but the
gristly white stubble on his face showed that he hadn't
shaved for days.

"What if I am?" She was trying to fumble the clasp
on the flap of her purse.

"If you're looking for a gun, you won't be needing
it. I'm Charlie Tate—the fellow you're supposed to
meet."

"Oh—" She licked her lips and forced a smile, but
wasn't quite ready to extend her right hand to him. "It's
nice to—to meet you, Mr. Tate."

"Call me 'Charlie'—everybody else does."

" 'Mary Frances'—I mean, that's what you can call me. Or 'M.F.,' if it suits better.''

"I like 'Mary Frances.' I had a daughter named Mary. Had a mule named Francis, for that matter. It didn't talk like the one in the movies, though. The daughter got married, and the mule died. I'll stick to 'Mary Frances' with you.''

"Okay," she said as she slowly nodded.

"Then let's go," Charlie Tate suggested.

"I thought we were meeting in the restaurant—" Mulrooney began.

"You wouldn't want to eat or drink anything in there. I've got some hamburgers in the plane. Kind of cold, but they're wrapped in tin foil—and a thermos of coffee.''

Mulrooney blinked twice. " 'In the plane'?" she asked. She gestured toward the rain, getting her arm wet for the trouble. The gray-and-green-striped awning leaked badly. "In weather like this?''

"Hell—no offense, ma'am—but hell, when I was prospecting up in Alaska right after the war, I flew planes in worse weather than this.''

"Which war?" she interrupted.

"The one against Hitler and the Japs—that war.''

"Oh—" Mulrooney said as she raised her eyebrows.

"I flew with Chennault and the Tigers over in China. Folks used to shoot at us to show how happy they were we were there, and sometimes they'd miss.'' Tate scrunched his cowboy hat lower on his head and started into the rain. "Hell—this ain't nothin' but a long drizzle,'' he shouted to her as he stalked across the parking lot.

Holding up her pant legs as she jogged beside him, Mulrooney began, "Wait a minute—you didn't say anything about any plane ride. If you have a plane, why the hell didn't you meet me at the airport?''

"This is the airport," Tate replied, and he spit tobacco juice into a puddle just as his left boot splashed into it.

She looked ahead of her. "My God—it is an airport!" She stared at a field, a single runway and a tower. There were no lights. "But you can't take off—"

"Sure as shootin' can, Mary Frances. Landing's always harder—any fool can get a plane up into the air with no trouble," and he kept walking.

"But I've got an overnight bag in the trunk of the car—" Mulrooney pleaded. She didn't relish the thought of flying in this rainstorm.

"Be safe enough. Nobody steals nothing around here, anyways."

"But I'll need clothes and—"

"You won't be gone past noon tomorrow. Can you make it 'til then?" He'd stopped walking.

"Well—yes, I guess. But—but—"

"It's foolish to stand in the rain talking when we can talk and fly same time."

Mulrooney stood her ground, both her heels together, pulled up to her full height in her little yellow rubber rain jacket. Water streamed down over the hood, making her nose wet. "Wait a minute! You said we would go out into the desert and you'd show me the Seven Golden Cities of Cibola—"

"I aim to, little lady. But we've got to fly there first."

"You said you were a prospector, not a pilot."

"What? You expect me to travel cross the desert a-walking with my burro like they do in the Westerns?"

"Well—" She realized her cigarette was a limp mass of tobacco and paper in the fingers of her left hand. She dropped it, rubbing the wet tobacco off her hand against the thigh of her jeans.

"Well?"

"Well—well, yeah, I did."

Charlie Tate shrugged. "You want to see them seven cities where the houses and streets and all is gold, or do you want to drive back to your hotel in the rain, Mary Frances?"

She licked her lips and shook her head.

"All right," she blurted. "But I'll warn you—I do have a gun."

He swung open his soaked leather coat and exposed the butt of a gun stuffed in his belt. "Yeah—me, too—" and he laughed. He started walking again.

"Shit—" Mulrooney muttered, but she started walking after him.

JOE CAPEZI ROLLED OVER and opened his eyes. Linda, her blond hair framing her face against the midnight blue of the pillowcase, was still asleep. He rolled onto his back and stared at the pattern on the wall made by the sunlight as it filtered through the blinds. He looked at the watch on his left wrist. It was 7:30 A.M.

He swung his legs over the side of the bed.

His father would kill him when he found out about the twelve million dollars. And his father would find out once the computer was fully accessed and the code broken.

He thought about it. No, his father wouldn't kill him. He'd relegate him to running a chain of dry cleaners or movie theaters and never trust him again. That would be worse, because everyone would know.

He picked up the bedside phone, punched a card into the card dialer and waited.

The phone rang three times. Jess Adolphi, sounding half-asleep, answered. "Hello?"

"Hello—it's Joe. Get out to the desert and bring in the kid—we're doing it."

There was a long pause, then, "Jeez, Joe, it's—"

"Bring in the kid—we do it. Today. Go get him—I want him now," and Joe Capezi clicked the phone dead, still holding the receiver. He looked behind him at Linda. Sunlight and shadow made bands of brightness and darkness across her breasts, across her face.

He stood up, setting down the receiver. Naked, he walked across the bedroom carpet and to the little Van Gogh on the far wall. He took the picture down, then thought for a moment, remembering the combination had just been changed. He worked the dial right, then left, then right, then drew up the recessed door handle and twisted, swinging the safe door open.

There was money, a lot of it—used bills in wrappers. There was a Colt Combat Commander in .38 Super and two extra magazines. There was a manila envelope. He took out the envelope, opened it and removed the folded note from inside—for this he used the tweezers from inside the safe. He shook the note on the tweezers, reading the words pieced together from newspaper and magazine clippings. "I want four million dollars in small bills. Tell you when, where. No money, hotel burned to ground, all people dead."

Carefully, wedging the note against the shelf in the safe, he folded it closed, then, still using the tweezers, placed it inside the envelope. His own prints were already on it—and so were those of the kid in the desert. He used the tweezers not to smudge the kid's prints. Nineteen. A doper. Two arrests in L.A. that didn't stick, for torching warehouses. Two years for extortion. The kid was perfect—an animal.

Joe Capezi closed the safe.

He was glad he'd got an early start—he wanted time to select his most comfortable suit, his most comfortable shoes.

He wouldn't want to lose them in the fire.

He put the Van Gogh back on the wall and glanced at

Linda. She was still sleeping, and the silk sheet hugged her hips and thighs. He wanted to get back into bed with her, but it was time to get ready. Today was going to be a big day. He started for the bathroom.

14

George had made bacon and eggs and toast and Dan Track had eaten. He sat now over a cup of coffee, on the veranda beside the pool. It was nearly eleven, but it was a lazy sort of day.

George, hair still wet from the pool, smoked a cigarette. "Why are you still doing this?" he asked.

"What do you mean?" Track responded absently. He opened the snap flap pocket of his dark-blue cowboy shirt and found his guillotine. He took one of the Cuesta-Rey Six-Ts from the table and snipped the tip.

"I mean, it was different with that deal with Johannes Krieger and the warheads. That's what got us both into working for Sir Abner and the Consortium. I pretty much figured you did it to keep the heat off me as the only survivor of the truck convoy. So okay, it took us a while, but we got Krieger."

"Let me ask you something," and Track lit the long, thin, dark cigar in the blue-yellow flame of his Zippo. "Why are *you* still doing it?"

"Well, you're still—"

"But that's not it. The money? Sixty grand a year and expenses, places like this to live when we're on assignment, the insurance companies picking up the tab?" Track motioned to the plush surroundings of the rented house in Miami.

"No—well, yeah, that's part of it." George nodded, stubbing out one Winston and lighting another. "Yeah, the money's good, but I'm a young guy. I liked it when I was in air-force intelligence. I felt like I was doing something positive, you know?''

Track nodded, exhaling a cloud of the gray smoke, watching it dissipate in the air. ''I'll tell you something. I like the hundred-and-twenty grand a year twice as much as you like the sixty grand.''

''Don't rub it in—''

''We'll get you a raise one of these days. And you're right—I got into it to keep your ass away from the FBI and the terrorists. But that day got me thinking, too.''

''About what? Terrorists?''

''Sure, terrorists—whatever you want to call them. A guy who hits an old lady over the head with a piece of pipe so he can steal her Social Security money is a terrorist, too. Just less ambitious. When I was in CID, man, I saw so much of that crap. Big-time thieves, petty thieves, murderers, guys croaking their wives, wives croaking their husbands, smugglers, dope rings—you name it, I saw it. That's why I quit, didn't even hang on for my full twenty. I'd had a bellyful of it. Every time Sir Abner came around and bought me a ridiculously expensive dinner and offered me a job helping track down terrorists and big-time criminals, I always turned him down. All I was seeing was the same shit I saw in the Army all those years. You hang around with scum, even tracking them down, you get to thinking like them, talking like them. And killing like them. Just like when I was a kid in the gangs on the South Side of Chicago. You become your environment. It eats away at you.''

''But—''

''Let me finish, George. Anyway, this Krieger deal comes along. Here's a guy who murders women and children, kills a general, then takes the guy's identity so he can commandeer U.S. equipment to help him steal a hundred five-hundred-kiloton warheads so he can take over the world. And he almost did. That's the real sick part. He almost did. And there we were, going after this son of a bitch. I felt good about it. I felt really good about it. Half the time I was scared shitless. Dodged more bullets than they used in World War II, I think. But I really felt good that I was working to stop that guy.''

George studied the glowing tip of his cigarette, then after an instant nodded.

"So, with this thing, working for the Consortium with Sir Abner, I'm working outside the law and inside the law at the same time. A unique opportunity, George. I can do stuff no cop can do, no fed can do, and Sir Abner's always there with the Consortium's muscle to keep the lid on while I get the job done. I can play by whatever rules I want. I can use the same rules the bad guys use and nail their asses to the wall." Track stood up, wiggling his toes in his loafers, looking down at his shoes, studying them a moment. "Remember the Lone Ranger? It's that whole idea, that maybe sometimes somebody has to say, 'Hey, this crap can't go on. But it's going to go on unless I try to stop it. Nobody's going to go after the bad guys in the world unless I do it.'" Track turned around and looked at his nephew, his dead sister's son. George had her eyes, nothing else. But it was enough. "You understand what I mean?"

"Should I say something enigmatic in Arapaho before I saddle the horses?"

"Arapaho." Track grinned. "Good—yeah. But I figure there are a lot of Kriegers out there. Maybe some of them even worse than Krieger was, God forbid. But maybe you and I going after them can make a difference. Every one we get is one less somebody else has to go looking for."

"That's why you're doing this? Working for the Consortium?"

Track shrugged, feeling almost embarrassed. "Yeah, I guess it is. But don't tell Sir Abner. If he ever figures I really want to do this, he'll cut my salary." He forced a laugh.

George stood up. He wasn't laughing. "Don't ever repeat this, Uncle Dan—because I'll deny I said it. I guess maybe I'm doing it for the same reason you are." And then George laughed. "Goes to show how stupid I am," and he stubbed out his cigarette and walked away.

Dan Track watched, saying nothing. He looked at his watch. Sir Abner Chesterton was sending a messenger by with some documents to read aboard the overseas flight. The guy should have arrived a while ago. Dan Track went back to his coffee, but just from the look of it, he could tell it was cold.

It was just 8:00 a.m. as Josh Culhane, his hair still wet from the shower, zipped the fly on his Levi's. He walked across the hotel room to the closet where he'd left the pair of brown Tony Llama cowboy boots. He took them back to the edge of the bed, sat down and pulled them on.

He looked at himself in the mirror—he hadn't finished buttoning his shirt. "Good, Josh, real good. Nothing like being wide awake," he told his reflection, closing two more buttons on the long-sleeved, Army-issue, gray-green shirt. He caught up his wallet, money clip, handkerchief, keys, lighter and two unopened packs of cigarettes, then remembered to check that he'd locked the suitcase containing his guns. He had.

He started for the door. . . .

The hotel coffee shop was more massive than some of the larger restaurants Culhane had seen. He saw Morrison at the far end, characteristically sitting with his back to a wall, occupying a red booth with a gold-colored table. The hostess started for him, but Culhane waved her aside, saying, "I'm eating with the gentleman over there," and he motioned in Morrison's direction.

"Hey, Josh—over here," Morrison called out a little too loudly.

Culhane nodded, grinned, waved—and hoped Morrison would hold it down. He reached the booth, sliding in almost directly opposite Morrison.

"What do you want to eat? It's on Thom, and in this place they serve breakfast, lunch and dinner twenty-four hours a day."

Culhane shrugged and set his cigarette down in an ashtray. "Breakfast."

"Hey, miss!" Morrison shouted.

Culhane tried to shrink back in his chair as the waitress started over. She handed Culhane a menu, then refilled Morrison's coffee cup.

Culhane didn't open the menu. "What kind of Danish do you have?" he asked.

"Assorted fruit filled—" the waitress began. Culhane caught the large gold crown emblazoned on the woman's apron. The Vegas Crown Hotel logo was everywhere, he'd noticed.

"Heat up three without nuts and without coconut. Give me some butter, some coffee and a large glass of orange juice. Okay?"

The waitress nodded, repeating the order as she scribbled it on her order pad. "I'll be back with your coffee in a minute."

"Thanks," and Culhane stubbed out his cigarette, lighting another one immediately. He always smoked a lot right after waking up—to get the nicotine level back to normal. Maybe Fanny was right, he thought—he should quit smoking.

"I was hoping you really would rip that guy's tongue out last night and ram it up his you-know-what—" Morrison laughed.

Culhane shrugged. "I lost my temper. You know how that can be."

"You didn't lose your temper. That was controlled. If you really had ripped his tongue out and done the rest of it, that would have been losing your temper. Trouble with guys your age—early thirties, right?"

"Right."

The waitress brought the coffee and left. Culhane started adding cream.

Morrison resumed. "Trouble with guys your age is you're too socially conscious. Hell, some guy deserves to get his ass kicked, then kick it, dammit."

"Right." Culhane grinned. "See the desert warrior yet this morning?" Culhane asked, changing the subject.

"Nope. But I saw the two of you go for an elevator ride together. You follow him last night?"

Culhane didn't answer for a moment, inhaled on his fresh cigarette and nodded. "Yeah, guess he's a guest here."

"Spotted a rod on him, didn't you—I saw the double take. I was watching."

"It might have been a gun. I don't know. Probably just some normal guy with a good suntan. Relax about him."

"You're the one who brought him up," Morrison said through a cloud of cigar smoke. "But that was just to change the subject away from last night and Aaron Flaherty."

"You are an astute observer of humanity, sir." Culhane laughed, bowing across the table to Ed Morrison.

"Called being a writer. Same affliction you've got, Josh."

Both of them laughed. The waitress brought the orange juice and the three Danish.

As Culhane started to butter the first Danish, he glanced at Morrison. "Just coffee?"

"All I can stand to look at this early in the morning. You're about to make me puke with those damned sweet rolls."

"Yeah, well—"

"Thom wants me to give a little speech about electronic gadgets—spook stuff."

"That should be interesting. He asked me to talk

about guns. Most of the guys know guns pretty well, but some of them don't, and sometimes it's obvious. At least to me it is.''

"What kind of gun do you think the desert warrior carries?" Morrison asked.

Culhane looked at his Danish, then across the table at Morrison. "Why, are we betting on this, or something? I don't gamble."

"Just an educated guess, one pro to another."

Culhane thought for a moment. "You're figuring he's from the Middle East, right?"

"Right." Morrison nodded, relighting his cigar.

"Okay—Beretta. Either the old 1951 single action or the 92SB."

"The 92SB, I bet—I mean, if I can say 'bet' without offending your sensibilities regarding gambling."

"Yeah," Culhane answered through a mouthful of Danish and warm butter. "You can say 'bet,' but only three times. Say it four times and I get offended."

"Bet—bet—bet—bet."

Culhane looked across the table at Morrison and grinned. "Go to hell," he said.

15

Dan Track picked up the phone, shooting his left cuff and checking the time. It was almost eleven-thirty. "Yeah, this is Track." He was on edge; the messenger with the documents was a half-hour late.

"Dan—Abner Chesterton."

"I was just thinking about you, Sir Abner. Your messenger hasn't shown up yet."

There was a silence on the telephone, and for a moment Track thought the line had been severed. "You might ring off with me," Chesterton finally said, "and ring up your friend Lew Wilson. If the messenger hasn't arrived yet, there might be good reason for it. The documents he was bringing you definitely tie the Israeli commando team we were up against to the syndicate known as the Malina. They specialize in violence. There is some evidence, scanty at this point, that they may be a terrorist arm of the KGB, or at least some of the individual gang cells. Some of the leaders may be KGB."

"The guys down here?" Track asked.

"Mostly Israelis, but criminals all. Some of them emigrated from the Soviet Union to Israel before getting in trouble there. If they were not just an isolated Malina cell, you and George are in great danger. It's rather like wiping out a traditional Mafia operation, then sitting around waiting for another Mafia faction to call. If that messenger—" Sir Abner Chesterton's voice stopped.

Track waited an instant, then worked the buttons a few times.

This time the line actually was dead.

The messenger was now over a half-hour late. Track set down the phone. It had taken the Malina the half-hour to beat or otherwise force the information from the messenger, the information on where he and George were staying.

"Shit!" Track shouted. He started across the living room, breaking into a dead run for his bedroom, shouting, "George! George—get a gun!"

Glass shattered behind him, but Track didn't look back. It would be the patio doors, kicked or shot in. He reached the stairs leading to the bedrooms and took them three at a time. More glass shattered behind him. "George!" he yelled.

He reached the corridor, turning right, flinging open his bedroom door. The windows of his room exploded as the gunners outside searched for a target, and the rug at his feet shredded in long lateral crosshatching strips as submachine-gun slugs ripped into it.

Track ran back the way he'd come, past the stairs, making for George's bedroom—and George's guns—on the other side of the house. "George!" he shouted. No answer came back, and he started to rage inside. If they had killed his nephew, he thought—"Bastards!"

The door to George's bedroom was all the way open.

Track snatched up a vase from a small round table that stood in the hallway opposite the bedroom and hurled it through the doorway. The vase disintegrated in midflight as another burst of silenced subgun fire tore across the room.

Track tossed the wine table through the doorway, then rolled in after it. The wine table was cut to splinters in midair as Track rolled to his feet. The solitary sub-gunner was wheeling toward him. Track pivoted on his right foot, and his left kicked at the elongated silenced muzzle of the Uzi subgun.

The subgun coughed toward the doorway, and Track heard a scream as he did a forward roll under the muzzle of the Uzi as it swung back on him. Coming up on the gunner's right side, Track hammered both fists into the man's midsection. His left elbow snapped left laterally, slamming into the inside right forearm of the subgunner, while his right hand smashed upward, palm open, the heel of the hand pushing into the base of his assailant's nose. The nose bone snapped, and Track drove it up and through the ethmoid bone and into the brain. The subgunner's wide-open stare revealed a mixture of pain and death as his body sagged backward. Track reached to the floor for the subgun, only then seeing who had died in the doorway—another of the hit team.

As Track started for the doorway to pick up the other subgun, the fallen gunner's body danced on the floor as slugs tore into it. Track fell back, catching himself with his left hand against the carpeted floor. He reached out and snatched a spare magazine for the Uzi from the man's web gear and shoved it into his belt as he back-stepped toward the open second-story window, firing a series of short 3-round bursts from the subgun to hold back the opposition.

Stopping at the dresser, he yanked open the top drawer with his left hand. His right grabbed George's Colt Combat Government .45 and the Smith & Wesson 469. He rammed both pistols into his belt—the space around his waistline inside his Levi's was getting crowded—and picked up a magazine for each and a shoulder rig for the Smith that held two 20-round extension magazines. With the shoulder rig over his left shoulder, he unleashed a burst from the Uzi and started for the window.

More subgun fire tore into the room from the hallway, and Track fired out the magazine in the Uzi toward the doorway, then scrambled toward the window as he rammed a fresh magazine up the butt.

At least his waistline was lighter, he thought.

He reached the window and looked out through the open sash, past the white curtains being sucked out by the breeze. Two men stood on the slightly pitched first-floor roof leading from the far side of the house.

He tucked back inside, firing a short burst at the door again, and loaded the Smith with a double-column magazine. Then he set down the Uzi, slipped George's shoulder rig across his back and holstered the Smith 469. Track loaded the Colt and rammed the pistol, cocked and locked, into his belt. Now he was ready.

Picking up the Uzi, he sent another short burst toward the doorway. This time a heavy volume of answering fire screamed back.

He started back to the window—the two rooftop gunmen were a known commodity, and the odds for success were probably greater. He didn't know how many men were in the corridor.

Where the hell was George? he wondered.

With the Uzi in his right hand and the .45 in his left fist, he craned his neck to look out the window. The two subgunners had halved the distance to his side of the house.

"Wonderful," he said aloud as he stabbed the Colt into his trouser band, awkwardly pushing up the thumb safety.

The silencer tube on the Uzi was still hot to the touch, but he worked at it, anyway, twisting it free of the threaded muzzle and tossing it to the floor. Silenced shots weren't what he wanted—maybe a lot of gunfire would attract the police.

Hearing a sound behind him, he wheeled, pumping the Uzi's trigger for two 3-round bursts, ripping a chunk out of the doorframe. His ears rang with the intense sound of the subgun fire; the subgunner who'd started through the doorway was out of sight again.

The tendons in Track's neck went taut and a shiver ran up his spine. He was between a rock and a hard place, he thought as he stabbed the Uzi through the window, firing it in a spray over the roofline. Answering fire hammered into the window frame, sending up a shower of splintered glass and wood slivers as Track edged back.

He looked straight out over the roof. It overhung the garden to the rear of the veranda. Beneath it, if he remembered correctly, was a flower garden, recently worked. The ground would be soft, and it was only a ten-foot drop, twelve at the most. He tried to recall if there were any metal stakes in the garden. He didn't think so, but he'd soon find out, he thought as he smiled.

He jabbed the Uzi through the window again and hosed the far side of the roof with a stream of slugs until the Uzi went empty. Tossing the subgun out the window, Track snatched at George's .45 with his right hand and threw his body through the raised sash onto the roof. Taking the impact with his left shoulder, he rolled down the incline, spread-eagling his legs as he skidded along the roof toward the edge, slowing himself, stopping, his left hand thrusting out to support his gun hand, his right thumb working down the Colt's safety.

He settled the sights on one of the subgunners stepping from the eaves on the far side of the house and pumped the Colt's trigger four times. The man's body twitched and lurched, and the Uzi in his hands sprayed wildly as he pirouetted like a dancer and tumbled over the edge of the roof, a choked scream coming from his throat.

Behind him he heard the crunching of broken glass under boots, coming through the open window of George's bedroom. He snapped the Colt to his right, his right arm fully extended, and fired the last rounds in the pistol. The flash of a face at the window became a splotch of red, and the face shattered and then disappeared from sight.

The Colt's slide locked open, and Track levered himself off the roof with his right hand, still clutching the pistol. There was a second of free fall, and he thrust his hands ahead of him, his legs twisting forward as he fell.

He landed, hands and knees, in the freshly dug garden. Two inches from his head was a spear-pointed steel spike rising eight inches from the dirt. He looked at the little white painted metal placard it supported. In green letters it read, Keep Off.

"You betcha—" Track muttered. He pushed himself up, shifting the empty Colt from his right hand to his left, and pulled the Model 469 Smith 9mm from the Bianchi Scorpio rig, working the slide-mounted safety up as he edged away from the garden.

He saw a sudden movement to his left, at the roofline. He fired without hesitation, and the second rooftop subgunner's Uzi sprayed wildly into the garden. Track jumped back, firing another 2-round semiautomatic burst with the little black Smith auto.

The subgunner's body seemed to hesitate, then leaned forward and fell, swan-diving from the roof.

Track set off in a run toward the pool near the front of the house. He was beginning to worry about George.

He kept running, hearing pistol shots from the upper floor of the house. He wheeled, pointing the little 9mm on line with an open upper-floor window, pumped the trigger and went back into a run.

The pool was ahead and to his right. Coming through the shattered glass doors leading back into the living room and the rest of the house were two men with Uzi subguns.

Track swung the Smith toward them, the sick feeling in his stomach telling him that at best he had maybe two shots left.

He started to fire.

There was a sudden roar, then another and another as more of the glass from the doors shattered, but outward this time. The two men with the Uzis were rocketed forward from the force of the blasts. One gunner stumbled into the pool, his gun discharging into the water. Then the body went beneath the surface and was gone.

The second man was still moving, intestines hanging out from his khaki shirt above his belt. He raised his subgun, and Track stroked the Smith's trigger—one shot, and the slide locked open. There was another of the familiar loud roars, and the subgunner's body lurched with the impact and sprawled forward. His head cracked sickeningly against the concrete lip of the pool, and the body lay still.

Track was snatching for one of George's spare magazines for the 469 when George stepped through what was left of the glass doorway. He held the SPAS in front of him.

"Where the hell were you?" Track demanded.

George shrugged. "I was taking a crap—you know how I am if I get constipated. Anyway, I killed the guy who came for me in the bathroom."

"I bet I know how—gas attack, right?" Track countered.

"I'll ignore that," George said as he grinned. "I took his gun and got the two guys in your bedroom. Then I got your guns. There's still about five of them upstairs, maybe six. Do you want to get them now or just hold them inside and wait for the cops?"

Track looked at George. "Swap weapons with me. You and I had better take them. No sense letting a bunch of local cops get themselves killed."

"Yeah, I was thinking the same thing," George added.

There were police sirens in the distance; this particular Miami suburb didn't have the best response time in the world, Track thought. But from the sound of the sirens, he judged he had between three and five minutes to deal with the remaining members of the hit team.

It would be enough.

He started up the stairs, crawling on knees and elbows. He'd sent George to the far side of the house to shinny up one of the trees and reach the front roof, then come in through the front bedroom opposite George's own room. He wanted to close the five men in a cross fire. Or maybe there were six, Track thought.

To Dan Track, well armed with the SPAS, the Metalife Custom L-Frame and the Trapper Scorpion, it didn't really matter. These men would die. All of them were guilty of past murders, robberies, kidnappings—and likely crimes he couldn't even catalog. It was like shooting rats in a garbage dump beside your house. Kill them before some night you awaken and they're gnawing at your toes.

Dan Track reached the top of the stairs, keeping his head just below the level of the hall floor. He held the SPAS, with its stock collapsed, ahead of him. He was waiting for George to open up with the two Uzis, the silencers removed from both. They would make enough noise to wake the dead.

As Track waited the sirens grew louder, and he judged them to be about two minutes away at the most.

He heard the crackle of a 9mm subgun repeat itself in continuous fire and he was up and running, firing the SPAS through the doorway of his own bedroom, firing it down the corridor to his left, firing it into the bedroom door opposite his room. Buckshot lacerated the walls and doorframes, and glass shattered as pellets strayed into unknown fragile targets.

He reached George's room. Two men confronted him, both armed with subguns. One was starting through the window onto the back roof. Track fired the SPAS, and the man's rear end took the load of buckshot. The force of the shot column at the distance of less than fifteen feet hammered the man out of the window. Track wheeled as the second subgunner brought his Uzi to bear. Track fired—once, twice, a third time. The

SPAS was empty, but the successive loads of double O buck threw the subgunner's body across the top of a dresser, into the mirror. The mirror cracked as the body slumped, rolled, then splayed out on the floor.

"Seven years bad luck for you, sport," Track growled as he let the SPAS fall on its sling to his right side. With his left hand—awkwardly, because shoulder holsters weren't really made to function that way— Track freed the Smith revolver. His right fist closed on the Trapper-modified Colt .45, his fingers curling around it, his thumb jacking back the hammer to full stand.

Subgun fire echoed from the room opposite him.

Track stepped toward the closed door, his right foot kicking out against the lock. The handle shattered, and bits of brass and metal fell to the carpeted floor as the door swung inward.

It was like a cut from a silent movie, Track thought, with the characters moving in slow motion. Three men were in the room, one of them rolling on the carpet toward the middle of the floor, firing an Uzi. Two more were crouched behind the bed. In the window frame he could see George, a subgun spitting fire from his right hand.

Track fired both pistols, catching one of the men behind the bed with a shot from both the .45 and the .357. The body, half turning toward him, lurched, then spread-eagled across the mattress.

The second man was rolling across the bed. Track shot him twice with the .45.

The third man was getting to his knees on the rug. Blood covered his chest, hands and neck. Track raised the .357 Magnum, but a burst from George's Uzi cut the man down.

Track stood still and remembered to breathe as George stepped through the window. "Dan—look out!" he yelled.

Track threw himself forward, below the muzzle line of George's subgun. The chatter of subgun fire crackled in the air both in front and behind him as he rolled onto his back, emptying the L-Frame toward the doorway while he double-actioned the trigger.

A subgunner stood frozen in the doorway. Then he fell backward into the corridor, his eyes open, dead.

"You all right?" Track yelled from the floor.

He looked behind him. George nodded, but his hands were shaking. George cleared his throat. "See, I told you there were six of them!"

" 'Maybe'—that's all you said. 'Maybe,' " Dan Track told him, forcing a laugh he didn't feel.

16

Mordecai Nitsch sat on the edge of his bed. He looked at his wristwatch. All of his team would be in place. He had already selected which one of his own men he would kill, then plant the incriminating documents on. It would be Moishe Sebin. That would take care of any feelings Charlene had for Sebin, once and for all. Charlene had left Odessa with him, Nitsch. They had emigrated as man and wife to Israel, and both had served in the Israeli armed forces, where they'd met Sebin and some of the others. Sebin was not Russian, but was criminally inclined, and Nitsch had brought him into the Malina, using the cover of their affiliation with the Israeli military for weapons thefts, smuggling and drug dealing. A KGB connection with the Malina had long been suspected by the Israeli military authorities and the Mossad, and when they began to close in, Sebin had accompanied Nitsch and Charlene to France. In France, with expensively purchased forged documents, all three had taken the identities of immigrants fresh from Soviet religious oppression in Russia, then obtained visas to the United States.

Sebin was the perfect setup—an Israeli by birth who had entered the United States with forged documents and overstayed his visa.

He was the perfect man to die with the Israeli documents planted on his body, Israeli documents made by the KGB.

Charlene would loathe Sebin's memory because Sebin, despite his criminality, had been a practicing

Jew. Charlene had recently become one. Nitsch, Jewish by birth, was an atheist. As he studied the Mini-Uzi he had retrieved from his car an hour earlier, he considered his lack of faith. Sometimes, he thought, it would be convenient to have a god of some sort to pray to, for success, for power in battle. But there was no such god available, no patron of criminal enterprise.

Sebin's death would have to solve it all.

It would bring Charlene back. It would bring U.S.-Israeli relations to an all-time low. It would fund KGB-Malina operations in the United States for some time to come. It might even get him past couriers like the beautiful blonde he knew only as Hummingbird, might even allow him to meet Potempkin, the covert-operations section chief for KGB activities in the United States.

He had worked for KGB all his adult life, informing on black market operations within the Soviet Union and at the same time promoting himself in the Malina organization because of the clever way in which his operations eluded authorities. He hoped Charlene would never find out about the KGB connection. The KGB had arrested and tortured her brother. Her brother had never been heard from again.

She was a criminal, apolitical and occasionally too softhearted. Nothing more. But her legs, when they wrapped around him. . . . He stood up and set down his gun. He walked to the closet and removed the khaki coat for his suit and returned with this to the bed, slung the Mini-Uzi from his right shoulder, then pulled on the coat. He looked at himself in the mirror. A sharp person would spot the miniaturized submachine gun; the average person would not. His stepping from the elevator would be the signal for the assault on the Vegas Crown hotel-and-casino complex to begin. He would not need to conceal the subgun for long.

He took his Beretta 92SB from the bed, placing it in the inside waistband holster he already wore at his right

1. How do you rate _____ ?
   (Please print book TITLE)

   1.6 ☐ excellent   .4 ☐ good   .2 ☐ not so good
   .5 ☐ very good   .3 ☐ fair   .1 ☐ poor

2. How likely are you to purchase another book in this series?

   2.1 ☐ definitely would purchase   .3 ☐ probably would not purchase
   .2 ☐ probably would purchase   .4 ☐ definitely would not purchase

3. How do you compare this book with similar books you usually read?

   3.1 ☐ far better than others   .4 ☐ not as good
   .2 ☐ better than others   .5 ☐ definitely not as good
   .3 ☐ about the same

4. Have you any additional comments about this book?

   _____ (4)
   _____ (6)

5. How did you *first* become aware of this book?

   8. ☐ read other books in series   11. ☐ friend's recommendation
   9. ☐ in-store display   12. ☐ ad inside other books
   10. ☐ TV, radio or magazine ad   13. ☐ other _____
   (please specify)

6. What *most* prompted you to buy this book?

   14. ☐ read other books in series   17. ☐ title   20. ☐ story outline on back
   15. ☐ friend's recommendation   18. ☐ author   21. ☐ read a few pages
   16. ☐ picture on cover   19. ☐ advertising   22. ☐ other _____
   (please specify)

7. Have you purchased any books from any of these series or by these authors in the past 12 months? Approximately how many?

	No. Purchased		No. Purchased
☐ Mack Bolan	(23) _____	☐ Clive Cussler	(49) _____
☐ Able Team	(25) _____	☐ Len Deighton	(51) _____
☐ Phoenix Force	(27) _____	☐ Ken Follet	(53) _____
☐ SOBs	(29) _____	☐ Colin Forbes	(55) _____
☐ Dagger	(31) _____	☐ Frederick Forsyth	(57) _____
☐ The Destroyer	(33) _____	☐ Adam Hall	(59) _____
☐ Death Merchant	(35) _____	☐ Jack Higgins	(61) _____
☐ The Mercenary	(37) _____	☐ Gregory MacDonald	(63) _____
☐ Casca	(39) _____	☐ John D. MacDonald	(65) _____
☐ Nick Carter	(41) _____	☐ Robert Ludlum	(67) _____
☐ The Survivalist	(43) _____	☐ Alistair MacLean	(69) _____
☐ Duncan Kyle	(45) _____	☐ John Gardner	(71) _____
☐ Stephen King	(47) _____	☐ Helen McInnes	(72) _____

8. On which date was this book purchased? (75) _____

9. Please indicate your age group and sex.

   77.1 ☐ Male   78.1 ☐ under 15   .3 ☐ 25-34   .5 ☐ 50-64
   .2 ☐ Female   .2 ☐ 15-24   .4 ☐ 35-49   .6 ☐ 65 or older

Thank you for completing and returning this questionnaire.

Y1234567

NAME _____
(Please Print)

ADDRESS _____

CITY _____

ZIP CODE _____

BUSINESS REPLY MAIL

FIRST CLASS   PERMIT NO. 70   TEMPE, AZ.

POSTAGE WILL BE PAID BY ADDRESSEE

NATIONAL READER SURVEYS

2504 West Southern Avenue
Tempe, AZ   85282

kidney. He placed spare magazines for the Beretta in the outside patch pockets of his suit coat. A Chiefs Special was already in place on his left ankle. Spare 32-round magazines for the Mini-Uzi were positioned in a row in his belt, starting from the center of his back and running to his left kidney—five in all. A 20-round magazine, shorter and more easily concealable, was in the subgun.

Nitsch started for the door, glancing at the Omega on his left wrist. Two minutes to nine. He should reach the lobby precisely at 9:00 A.M.

He let the hotel-room door slam closed behind him, never looking back. Removing fingerprints from the room would have been an exercise in futility. The room, like the entire hotel, would be completely destroyed when they activated their explosives.

He pressed the elevator call button. The elevator doors opened, and he stepped in, thinking that he was stepping into history.

JESS ADOLPHI CLUTCHED THE ARMRESTS of the copilot's seat in the twin-engine Beechcraft Baron, alternating his gaze from the pilot's hands to the floor beneath his own feet. He couldn't bring himself to look through the windshield. Takeoffs and landings in large commercial jetliners terrified him. The business jet his boss, Joe Capezi, so often used, frightened him even more. But he was usually able to calm his nerves with a glass of whiskey. This thing was something else again. "How soon before we land?" he asked the pilot.

"Jess, for a bodyguard, somebody who runs around carrying guns and all that, man, you're the biggest chicken shit I've ever seen." Tal Kelly laughed.

"Yeah, well, you land this sucker in one piece fast and stop circling the damn desert. Come on—please!" Adolphi pleaded.

Tal Kelly was looking at him, laughing. "I was only

circling to find the safest spot to touch down, but if you don't care about safety—''

"So circle already, but get us down!" Jess Adolphi looked back at his shoes and tried thinking of something other than flying. The plan for the next piece of the operation was well worked out. They would land, then walk over to the old house in the desert where they had the crazy kid chained up like some kind of animal. Pete, who had guarded the kid for the past five weeks—he must be stir crazy by now, Jess Adolphi figured—had to be killed. Adolphi looked at Tal Kelly. He would have to be killed, too, but not until they got the kid back to the airport outside Las Vegas. Not until they were safely on the ground.

Adolphi looked back to his shoes. He wondered if Joe Capezi had already slotted someone to have him—trusted Jess who did everything—murdered. "No—" He said the word aloud.

" 'No' what? You know, Beechcraft makes one of the safest planes in the world. Relax," Kelly said.

"I wasn't talking to you," Adolphi answered, forcing a smile.

He could feel the aircraft settling into an approach. He had ridden in it enough.

When he got off the plane, he'd add one small item to the plan—he'd throw up. And then he'd feel better—about everything.

ED MORRISON AMBLED OUT of the hotel men's room, his stomach feeling only slightly better. The diarrhea had been constant for the past several weeks, and only by limiting his food intake to things that were as bland as possible and increasing his fluid intake had he been able to keep going. But the additional fluids only aggravated the diarrhea. The vitamin tablets were what kept him alive, he thought.

He felt the fear welling up in him, fear of going to the doctor. Cancer. It had to be.

He walked as hurriedly as his aching body would allow. Josh Culhane had been about to give his talk on the firearms the various writers armed their heroes with, and he did not want to miss that. Culhane was a good boy—he wrote well; he wrote truthfully. That was saying a lot. When Culhane's twin brother, Jeff, had died, Morrison had thought it might have pulled Josh Culhane's plug. Josh had dropped from sight for a few weeks—he had never explained why beyond saying he and Mary Frances Mulrooney had gone on a trip. But Josh had bounced back and still wrote well.

Morrison turned the corner past the elevator banks, heading toward the conference rooms beyond, when he pulled himself to an abrupt halt. In front of him stood the suntanned man with the dark wavy hair, still wearing his khaki suit—the man he and Josh Culhane jokingly referred to as the "desert warrior." Maybe Culhane was right, Morrison thought. Maybe he was paranoid.

But there was no mistaking the outline he saw under the right armpit of the desert warrior's coat. It was a submachine gun.

"Oh, fuck," Morrison grunted.

Less than a yard from him, Morrison saw one of the uniformed security police. If he tried to warn the man, the desert warrior would have time to get the subgun into action, killing the policeman and some of the other people moving past the elevator banks.

Morrison laughed—if cancer were eating his insides apart, he'd rob it of the final victory, maybe. "Go down shooting," he growled under his breath.

He turned to the security officer and noticed the Border Patrol rig the officer wore. His gun was a stainless-steel K- or L-Frame Smith, and Morrison knew it would be loaded with .38 Specials. It would do the job he had in mind.

"Hey, officer—can I ask you a question?" Morrison called out, lighting a cigarette.

Under his breath, looking at the desert warrior, he muttered, "Won't expect it from an old fart like me."

As the security officer approached, Morrison saw the desert warrior make eye contact with someone on the casino floor.

"Yes, sir," the security officer said as he smiled.

Morrison bent toward him. "Your zipper's down, sonny."

The security officer immediately moved his hands forward, toward his crotch. Morrison's left hand shot out toward the holster, while his right hand fastened on the guard's carotid artery at the angle of the jaw from the neck. His fingers applied the pressure technique a Japanese Ninja instructor had taught him years ago in Osaka, and the security officer started to collapse. He would be unconscious or nearly that for less than thirty seconds. Morrison had given the touch only lightly. With a harder pinch the man would have been dead in twelve seconds.

Morrison's left hand held the butt of the revolver, while he worked the holster's safety strap open with his thumb.

There was no time to shift the revolver into his right hand—the desert warrior was already turning in his direction as the security officer sank to the floor. The desert warrior's coat flew open, and a Mini-Uzi stabbed outward.

Morrison stamped his left foot as he thrust the left leg forward and pulled the trigger of the Smith revolver once, twice. The third pull was nearly through as the Mini-Uzi opened up. Morrison felt the bullets rip into his already-aching insides as his third shot went into the floor. He doubled forward, losing his balance, then crashed to the floor, his hands clutching his stomach. As he went down, he saw the desert warrior clutch the upper portion of his left thigh, blood spraying from between his fingers.

There was gunfire all around him now as Morrison's head snapped against the carpeted floor. His mind lost touch with his body, and he couldn't move, but he laughed under his breath, feeling the salty taste of blood in his mouth. "Damn gun shot low—so'd the shooter—" And then his world turned black.

17

Soundproof rooms made him nervous—at least Josh Culhane told himself that it was being in a soundproof conference room, isolated from the outside world that was doing it. Thom Hark had just asked him to address the issue of firearms selection.

Hark smiled, saying, "Ed isn't back yet, I know—but we have a great deal to cover here today, and we want to be through in time for dinner and the show tonight."

"Who are we seeing?" Bob Meadowshed asked.

"Engelbert Humperdinck, actually," Hark replied sheepishly.

No one said anything. Then Hark looked at Culhane again. "Ed's one of the few men here who knows as much about firearms as you do, Josh, so he's among the least likely to suffer from missing part of your talk."

"All right." Culhane nodded, forcing a smile. He looked around the three sides of the rectangle where his fellow adventure writers were seated—some of the faces he knew well, some very little. On the fourth side of the table Thom Hark sat with one of the corporate vice-presidents and one of the marketing men. Publishing, Culhane reflected, was like that these days. "All right," Culhane said again. "Thom asked me to put together a few remarks on guns. So here goes. Not one of you—us—can be criticized for some of the things some writers from other publishing houses can be criticized for. In other words, putting safety catches on revolvers, even though the French police have some revolvers especially made with safety catches, or having a pistol with a 7-round magazine fire twenty rounds without reloading. Everybody has apparently done his homework on the guns he's selected for his characters to use. And that's fine—but this is something Thom and I have talked about occasionally on the telephone. Some of the guns some of you pick just wouldn't make it in real life. For example—'' and he looked directly at Aaron Flaherty ''—Aaron Flaherty's character Deke Cutter. No professional in his right mind these days, no matter how sentimentally attached he was to a gun, is going to carry a .32 Smith & Wesson Long revolver in a Bianchi 9R upside-down rig. The holster is fine—I've used them for real, but with a .38 Special revolver or a stubby-barreled .357 Magnum. Why waste all that leather for such a next-to-useless caliber?''

Flaherty interrupted. ''Deke Cutter needs a small caliber gun—he's low profile all the way,'' he protested.

''Fine,'' Culhane replied. ''Then get him one of the new Smith J-Frames with the 3-inch barrel and fixed sights in .22 Magnum. That's a small caliber and—'' Culhane stopped in midsentence as the door behind him burst inward. The door slammed closed just as quickly, but not before two men, Uzi submachine guns in their hands, had entered the room.

In a very thick Com-bloc accent, the man to Culhane's left snarled, ''No one moves! Hands in the air—quick!''

Josh Culhane looked over his shoulder at Thom Hark and the two publishing-company executives. They were starting to raise their hands.

Culhane looked to his right; Bob Meadowshed's eyes were darting back and forth, but his hands weren't raised. Flaherty's hands were above his head, but they were steady—Culhane gave him that. At the far corner of Culhane's side of the table was Ralph Dolore. He had been quiet the previous night, quiet that morning. Now his face was expressionless. He was a good writer. His hands hadn't raised, either.

"Hands up! Now, or we'll shoot," the vocal one of the two subgunners reiterated.

Culhane looked at them and laughed, as he walked toward them slowly. "Ed Morrison—he put you guys up to this, didn't he?" he asked. "They're making those replica models real good these days—those Uzis look the genuine article."

The talkative subgunner took a step closer to Culhane, thrusting the Uzi forward into a hard assault position. Culhane turned half right, as if to look at Thom Hark, Bob Meadowshed and the others. He pushed up on his right toe, his left leg snaking out in a double tae kwon-do kick, tapping into the muzzle of the subgun, knocking it to the floor. Planting his left foot, Culhane pivoted, his right leg extending, his right hand gently pushing into the chest of the second man, knocking him into the doorframe. Culhane snatched up the fallen Uzi, his right fist closing over the pistol grip, his right index finger slipping into the trigger guard.

The subgun was aimed between both men. "Now Ed's a hell of a guy. But I don't like anybody pointing guns at me—real or pretend," Culhane said sternly.

Culhane eyed the two men, smiling. "Sorry, guys—I didn't mean to get rough," and Culhane removed the magazine from the subgun. "Works just like the real thing." He laughed, noticing the second man, his body pushing away from the doorframe, the Uzi going to an assault position. "Hey—enough's enough, huh?" Culhane looked at the top of the 32-round magazine. What he saw in the double-column box was real ammo. "Holy shit!" he yelled.

The second subgunner was moving, swinging the

muzzle of his Uzi around. Culhane, not having time to
ram the stick back up the well of the Uzi, thrust the
empty subgun toward the disarmed man. But he wasn't
quite disarmed, Culhane realized as he saw the man
reaching for a semiautomatic pistol with his right hand.
The man stumbled back, and Culhane's right arm arced
toward the face of the still-armed subgunner. Culhane's
fist, holding the ejected magazine, crashed against the
left side of the subgunner's face, and a burst of 9mm
bullets pelted into the ceiling as the second-man's head
snapped back.

Culhane threw himself against the gunner, shouting,
"Somebody get the other guy!"

Culhane dropped the magazine and moved both of
his hands to the subgunner's throat, his right knee
smashing up into the man's groin. Across his opponent's back he could see Bob Meadowshed and the quiet
guy, Ralph Dolore, disarming the first man. Culhane
snapped the second subgunner away from the wall. His
left fist bunched on the man's clothes; his right hammered forward, impacting the center of the face.

He let go of the man's clothes, and the body fell at his
feet. Culhane reached to the floor, picking up the Uzi
the man had dropped when Culhane had kneed him.

Hark crossed from the far side of the room and
picked up the emptied Uzi. Culhane found the ejected
magazine and tossed it to him. "You know how to use a
gun?" he asked.

"I've handled a Sten—you can't expect much more
than that from someone who was born in England and
lives in Canada."

"You're right," Culhane agreed as he surveyed the
scene.

Meadowshed had taken a pistol from the first man,
and Flaherty had joined them at the door—he was ac-
tively searching the second man. Both the invaders were
unconscious. "Anybody here really good with a sub-

gun?'' Meadowshed asked, holding up an Uzi. "I'm a pistol man myself. I've used these things from time to time, but I'm better with a handgun."

He turned to Ralph Dolore. "Here—" and Dolore extended a pristine-condition F.I.E. TZ-75, the Italian version of the Czech CZ-75 double-column-magazine 9mm. "I'm good with a subgun," Dolore said. Culhane thought that Dolore was almost going to smile as he handed him the Uzi, taking the TZ-75 and two spare magazines. He stuffed these in his Levi's pockets.

Culhane's right fist closed around the smooth wooden stocks. His thumb pushed the Colt-Browning-type magazine release catch. The 15-round magazine seemed full. He edged back the slide—there was a round chambered.

He left the safety off, the hammer down for a first shot. "Let's check the corridor—unless these guys just came to frighten us, there should be more of them," he suggested.

"What about Ed Morrison?" Thom Hark asked.

Culhane looked at the Englishman and nodded in the direction of the two assailants. "These guys probably have something to do with why Ed never got back. If there's trouble out there, Ed isn't the kind of guy to avoid it." He glanced at Bob Meadowshed. "You and Ralph—" and he gestured to Dolore holding the subgun "—you two guys are one team. Thom and I will be the other. Once we hit the corridor, do just what we have the guys do in the books—fire-and-maneuver elements. Thom and I will go first."

"Thanks a lot, Josh." Hark laughed sourly.

"Yeah, I knew you'd like it. Riding that desk up there in Toronto all the time, when your body and soul are craving action—well, crave no longer."

"My thought exactly." Hark nodded. "There may not be anything left to crave with."

"Hmm." Culhane shrugged, then opened the door into the corridor. The effect was like turning on a radio program from days gone by. The sounds of gunfire were everywhere; the wail of police sirens was distant but distinct; screams and shouted curses filled the air.

Culhane edged through the cracked doorway, while Hark followed slightly behind. As they listened to the action around them, Culhane decided that the greatest amount of gunfire was coming from the casino and the main lobby.

Culhane readied himself to cross the corridor, whispering to Thom Hark, "Cover me."

Culhane sprinted the twelve feet to the other side of the hallway, flattening himself against the far wall. Somebody handed two more magazines to Thom Hark through the doorway, and Hark jammed them into his trouser belt. He let out a groan. "That's damned uncomfortable," he rasped to Culhane. "Your Sean Dodge does that all the time with submachine-gun magazines—"

"He wears a wider belt," Culhane shot back.

"Bullshit. Where are we going?"

"To find Ed Morrison. Remember, we're the good guys. Move out." Culhane started forward, the TZ-75 raised in his right hand beside the corridor wall, Hark moving nearly parallel to him on the other side of the hall, the subgun held in an assault position. Culhane wondered if Hark had more experience than he let on.

They had halved the distance from the conference room to the end of the corridor when Culhane glanced back. Bob Meadowshed and Ralph Dolore were advancing, as well, about twenty yards back. Dolore gripped an Uzi like an old friend, while Meadowshed held on to a Browning Hi-Power 9mm. Behind Meadowshed were the other half-dozen writers. Aaron Flaherty was holding a knife taken from one of the two unconscious subgunners. The others were variously armed, and Culhane noticed another knife, a belt held like a garrote, one of the metal folding chairs from the conference room and a Frisbee-sized glass ashtray. We're sure not going to overwhelm them with a display of our firepower, he thought as he looked ahead again. He wished he were with Fanny Mulrooney in the desert, looking for her Seven Golden Cities of Cibola. He asked himself what his fictional adventure hero Sean Dodge would do, and answered his own question—hit and run, to hit and run again.

Culhane pulled up by the end of the corridor. The rattle of subgun fire had nearly stilled, but the sounds of human misery continued in a litany of terror with screams, men and women crying and groans of agony. A voice boomed over the PA system, and Culhane froze, recognizing it. "All resistance has been crushed. Any attempt to interfere with our robbery of the casino will result in instantaneous execution. The police are outside. If they attempt to storm the casino, all hostages will be killed. All doctors and other medical personnel are to report to the blackjack tables on the far wall immediately." It was the voice of the desert warrior, but the voice was strained, as though the man were in severe pain.

Culhane moved ahead to the two wide doors used to close off the corridor. One of them was propped open, and he edged beside it and peered through the opening.

The first thing he saw was Ed Morrison's lanky frame being carried by wrists and ankles between two of the subgun-armed attackers and two frightened-looking men dressed as croupiers. Morrison's white shirt was stained red with blood.

Culhane's stomach churned as Morrison was unceremoniously dumped on top of one of the crap tables.

Culhane waited—if a doctor was going to attend Morrison, he didn't want to interfere. Culhane made a decision then and there—if these men had killed Morrison, he'd kill them.

Thom Hark had edged up beside him. "My God!" he exclaimed.

"Yeah," Culhane whispered.

18

"We have located two doctors and five nurses. One of the nurses is an employee of the hotel," Moishe Sebin told Mordecai Nitsch.

Nitsch nodded, happy for once at Sebin's presence. Sebin was competent, and after the older man had shot him twice in the upper left thigh, Sebin had reorganized the attack within moments and triumphed. But gunfire had not been part of the plan. Men had been stationed everywhere throughout the lobby and the casino and were even now taking over the executive floors. Having taken over the hotel switchboard, there was to have been no gunfire to attract police.

More sirens screamed outside as police and emergency vehicles swarmed to the front of the hotel.

"Fuck this," Nitsch snarled.

Charlene's hands were on his neck, rubbing it. "Rest easy, Mordecai, the doctor—"

Just then, some of Nitsch's men hustled a harried-looking group of men and women up to Nitsch's side. A tall, well-tanned, older man stepped forward, shaking himself free of two of Nitsch's men, and stated, "I'm a doctor. What do you want?"

A second man stepped forward and said, "I'm a doctor, as well. If you wish us to treat the injured, of course we—my colleague and I shall do that."

"I wish you to treat me first," Nitsch groaned.

The second doctor—short, stocky, dressed in a rumpled gray suit, a striped tie at half-mast beneath his double chins—stepped toward Nitsch. He looked at Sebin. "I'll need a knife to cut away the pant leg."

Sebin looked at Nitsch, and Nitsch nodded wearily. "Give him a knife," he said. Then he stabbed the muzzle of his Beretta 92SB toward the doctor and warned, "If you attempt to use it to harm me—"

"Smart move." The doctor nodded. "Threaten your doctor with death—very clever." He took the knife from Sebin and cut along the outer seam of Nitsch's blood-stained trouser leg. "You got a bleeder—at least one of them," he said. The rumpled gray doctor turned away. "You five ladies are all nurses? RNs?"

The women nodded or voiced verbal agreement. The doctor pointed to one of the women. "You—get some compression on these gunshot wounds, usual hand pressure to slow the arterial bleeding," he ordered, then started to walk away.

"Where the hell are you going? I need a doctor, not a nurse!" Nitsch demanded.

The doctor gestured to the gaming hall. "There's a man on that crap table who's got severe bleeding and whose intestines are hanging out. There's a woman with half her left leg shot off. There's a bellboy with a sucking chest wound. I've got bigger fish to fry. I'll be back to you later."

Nitsch cocked the hammer on the 92SB. "No, you won't," he shouted.

"Shoot me, then—and bleed to death."

Nitsch pointed the Beretta at the first doctor, the tall, well-tanned man. The doctor just grinned and said, "You can shoot me, too, then."

Nitsch watched helplessly as the rumpled doctor walked toward the man on the crap table. "That bastard shot me!" Nitsch screamed after him.

The stocky medical man turned around and looked at Nitsch. "Good for him!" he said.

WHEN HIS JAW DROPPED, the cigar fell from between his teeth onto the new green blotter near the center of his desk. Joe Capezi started to speak, retrieving the cigar, but one of a group of three men, each armed with submachine guns, spoke first. "Be still with your hands now!"

It was a hit—his father was having him hit. "Wait a minute! Whatever you're being paid, I'll double it—triple it. You name a figure—"

"Silence!"

"How much, damn it!" And he hammered his fists on the desk.

Through the open door he could hear gunfire. "What the hell are you doing?" he demanded. "Icing the whole goddamned hotel?"

If they were his father's trigger men and they hadn't killed him yet, then why wouldn't they take a bribe? he thought. "Who are you? Who—" he demanded.

The muzzle of a subgun bore down on him.

His palms were sweating suddenly, and he raised his hands high above his head. "Don't shoot, huh?"

A fourth armed man entered the room, dragging Milton, the accountant and computer expert, by the lapels of his jacket. The fourth man threw Milton half across the room, said something in a language Capezi couldn't understand and two of the original three men left with him.

The one who had spoken was the only one who remained.

"What's happening, Mr. Capezi?" It was Milton, on his knees on the floor between Capezi's desk and the man with the subgun. The man with the subgun closed the door with a back kick. "What's—"

The man with the gun cut Milton off. "Silence—total!"

Very slowly Capezi started to lower his hands.

"No! Up! Stand up!" the intruder ordered.

Capezi obeyed.

"Move over here—now you will!"

The guy's English was funny, Capezi thought. Who were they? Capezi walked around the desk and stood in front of it.

"Now you—up!" the subgunner ordered Milton.

"Yes, sir," Milton said as he nodded and moved to a standing position, raising his hands.

"Both men—take off belts!"

Capezi started to remove his belt. He was wearing a gun threaded to it in a flat silhouette belt holster. And the door was closed. He usually didn't wear the one gun he owned, but today he had; he'd planned to silence Jess Adolphi after Jess returned from the desert with the crazy kid. The .38 Super Colt Combat Commander was cocked and locked—Adolphi had told him that was the best way to carry the gun.

Joe Capezi reached for it, at the same time darting behind Milton, letting the accountant's body shield him from his opponent.

The submachine gun crackled, and Milton screamed as his body twitched under the impact of the 9mm slugs. But Capezi had the .38 Super Colt in his right hand and fired again and again and again until the action locked open.

Capezi found himself on his knees, with Milton bleeding to death against his chest.

The man with the submachine gun was dead.

"Mr. Capezi—you—" Milton began.

Capezi interrupted him, and his voice surprised him with its steadiness. "These guys did us a favor, Milton. When I torch the place, even my father will blame them. Too bad—" He was thinking of Milton. The eyes suddenly stopped flickering and there was a rattling sound from deep inside Milton's frail body.

Milton was dead.

"Too bad for you—but I would have had to kill you, anyway, Milton. Too bad, huh?"

Capezi didn't consider himself a cruel man, and, very gently he eased Milton's head to the floor, then set down his pistol. He found the spare magazines in his desk drawer and reloaded the Colt. Only then did he go back and kneel beside Milton again to thumb his eyes closed.

He stood up, walked over to the dead man and searched him, taking his submachine gun and two spare magazines.

He eased open the door leading from his soundproof office and looked out. The secretary's desk was empty.

Near the elevator bank, to his left, he could see one man on guard. Farther down, near the accounting office, he could see another man. But the door to the master accounting room was wide open, and he could see bodies on the floor.

It was unnerving. He closed the door. These guys hit us for the dough. Shit—he thought. He locked the door to the corridor, not knowing if that was wise or not.

There was a helicopter on the far end of the penthouse patio, tethered against the high winds that sometimes came in from the desert. He could fly it well, too. He was good at it.

Instead of walking to freedom through the shattered glass doors leading to the patio, he moved behind the bar and poured himself a short Jim Beam, then set the open bottle down. He twisted the ball-shaped finial on the top of the mirror-backed glassware cabinet and stepped back. The cabinet began to slide to his left, revealing a set of brushed-aluminum double doors.

He looked back to the bar and picked up a very old bottle of Dom Perignon. He broke the seal and thumbed up the cork.

There was no spray of the premium champagne.

He inverted the bottle in his hands, over the top of the bar.

Out of the mouth of the bottle poured an elevator key.

Setting the bottle on the bar, he walked through the opening in the wall and inserted the key into the lock plate near the top of the double aluminum doors and turned it.

There was a reassuring hum, and the doors parted with a pneumatic hiss.

He stepped inside and pressed the door button. The doors closed. He set the car in motion, toward the subbasement where he'd planned that the fire would start in the main elevator shafts.

"Burn the place down—and get those bastards with the submachine guns, too," he told his distorted reflection in the gleaming metal of the inside of the elevator doors.

He could already feel the motion in his stomach. The elevator plunged downward.

19

"The good thing about a single-engine aircraft," Charlie Tate shouted over the intermittent roar of the engine, "is that when they go out, a body can usually glide her down easy."

M.F. Mulrooney sat barefoot, her shoes still drying, in what would have been the copilot's seat if there had been any instrumentation. The rain had been localized, and none was falling now as they flew over the desert. "Are you telling me we're having engine trouble?"

"No such thing, Mary Frances—I just wanted to re-assure you and all. She's humming like a bumblebee, old Patsy is."

" 'Patsy'?"

"Named the plane after a burro I had 'round the same time I had Francis, the mule that didn't talk. Patsy was my dog."

"I thought you just said she was your burro."

"Well, she was a burro, but she was the color of an old yellow dog, so I named her like she was a dog and treated her like she was a dog. Even taught Patsy to fetch a stick now and again."

"What happened to Patsy?" Mulrooney asked.

"She died, 'round the same time Francis did. They was close. Grief got her, I think," and he looked away, his gray-blue eyes sparkling.

Mulrooney felt the sinking feeling in her stomach as the plane banked sharply. Charlie Tate said, "I always come at the old place out of the sun so no one can see.

The Japs used to love doing that over China. They'd
come at you—''

''I don't understand—''

''Light-colored plane, light-colored sky—they blend.
And it's a good thing I did,'' Tate said as he leaned for-
ward and peered intently through the windscreen.
''Somebody's there who ain't supposed to be there!''

''What?''

''You just look for yourself, Mary Frances,'' and
Tate nodded toward the distance.

M.F. Mulrooney leaned forward and peered through
Patsy's dirty windshield.

Perhaps a half mile to their left, she wouldn't have
bet on the distance, was a twin-engine aircraft in the
basin of a long, wide terrain feature she labeled a valley
but guessed had some other, more Western-sounding
name. On a rise beyond the valley and slightly to the
right of the plane was a small house that looked like a
shed, a pickup truck and a large travel trailer, the wheels
removed and the trailer mounted on blocks. Parked beside the travel trailer was a black sedan.

''The old pickup's mine, the trailer's mine—hell, even
the shed I built with my own two hands,'' Charlie Tate
told her. ''But that plane sure ain't mine—can't afford
a twin and don't want one. And that black Chevrolet
ain't mine, either. Looks like we've got some tres-
passers. But I aim to fix that,'' he said and the aircraft
banked again, climbing. ''Mary Frances—reach back
there and get me that guitar case,'' he ordered.

She looked at him, then twisted around in her seat.
On the flooring of the fuselage behind her was an olive-
drab back pack, a gasoline can lashed to the side of the
fuselage and a blue imitation-alligator-skin guitar case.
The handle had broken off and a piece of wire wrapped
in black electrical tape had taken its place.

As she made to lift the case, she realized it was terribly heavy. She half dragged it forward, stubbing her right big toe on the support for Charlie Tate's pilot's seat. "Ouch!" she exclaimed.

"Somethin' wrong, Mary Frances?"

"Oh, no, never mind. What's in the case, anyway? It's awfully heavy for a guitar!"

"Tommy gun—out here on the desert don't pay to take no chances."

"You mean you have a submachine gun in here?"

"You bet. General Chennault issued us weapons if we hadn't brought our own. Figured the one with the biggest hole in the front was the best, so I got me this here .45," and he slapped at his midsection and the butt of his pistol. "When things started gettin' a little violent over there, some of us got the chance to pick up a Tommy gun. After the war and all, I didn't see no sense in gettin' used to nothing else. And the Tommy gun has a big hole, too," and he laughed.

"What are you going to—"

"Had me a biker gang out here once—you shoulda seen 'em hightail it like jack rabbits some mountain lion wanted for a snack. Old Patsy an' me come in out of the sun with the Tommy gun blazin' to beat hell."

She opened the guitar case on her lap. Inside was a Thompson submachine gun packed with a drum magazine. There were also three stick-shaped magazines. "But maybe whoever owns that car is just some lost traveler—" she suggested.

"'Some lost traveler'! Hell—no offense—" The plane had leveled off and was banking toward Mulrooney's side again. "But no plane made can haul a black Chevrolet after it. Maybe it's a drug deal, or something. But we'll bust 'em up."

"You didn't say you were taking me along to go after people with a submachine gun. What about the—"

"Seven Golden Cities of Cibola? What do you think the trailer is parked over, Mary Frances?"

"You mean—" she began.

"There's a tunnel that starts under the trailer. Other tunnels spread off in a hundred different directions from it. I'm the only one what knows which tunnel leads into the caverns where the Seven Cities are."

"But—"

"Mary Frances, you just stick one of them magazines—not the drum, but one of the other ones—up the magazine well of that Tommy gun. The little rounded bullet part points toward the—"

"I know it points toward the front! The man I live with—boy, he could tell you a thing or two about guns. He's—"

"Just hand me the Tommy gun, Mary Frances." The plane was starting down out of the clouds now, and she could feel it in her ears and in the pit of her stomach. She handed him the Thompson.

He reached down to his door handle, twisting it, and the door, hinged at the rear, opened back.

Mulrooney checked her own door. "Why does this door open to the front?" she asked him.

"Don't need to fire a Tommy gun through it, so there wasn't any use changing it." Tate's door was open about a foot and secured with a latch at the top.

The plane was still descending as Charlie Tate worked the bolt on the submachine gun and prodded the muzzle out the door. "You just watch out for flying cartridge cases, Mary Frances," he warned.

"This is insane!" she cried at him. "You can't just strafe people from the air!" She could see the travel trailer and the little unpainted barnwood shed and the black, dust-covered Chevrolet. Off in the direction of the twin-engine plane, she could see three men and something else, something that looked like a man but was chained at the neck.

As Charlie Tate leveled off, the man leading the chained figure fell to the sand. Her eyes flashed to the other two men. One of them held a pistol. "He just murdered that other man!" she yelled over the engine noise.

"Told you they weren't just travelers, Mary Frances. Now hold the yoke and don't touch nothin'."

She looked into Charlie Tate's faded blue eyes, then nodded, reaching out with her left hand, holding the yoke.

"Keep her steady, Mary Frances—" he said, and the Thompson submachine gun opened up. A trail of tiny dust devils ate their way across the sand toward the two men.

"I ain't gonna kill that fellow they've got chained up. Maybe I won't kill none of 'em, just get 'em, and I can radio the police to come."

The two men Charlie Tate was closing in on started to run; one, wearing a Windbreaker and sunglasses, toward the twin-engine plane and the other, dressed in a suit and holding a pistol in his right hand, toward the trailer. He was the one who had shot the third man. He turned, near the trailer, raising the pistol, firing. The windshield in front of Charlie Tate's face cracked. There was another long burst of submachine gunfire, and Mulrooney's cheeks and nose and ears felt the hot brass as it pelted her flesh.

Beneath her, the man with the pistol went down as if somebody had yanked a rug out from beneath his feet.

The one running toward the twin-engine aircraft threw his hands into the air and stood rock still.

Mulrooney looked at Charlie Tate.

The Thompson submachine gun rested across his lap. On his chest was a growing splotch of dark blood.

As she screamed, he grabbed the yoke from her, coughing, blood spraying the windshield in front of him. His left hand clasped his chest, blood oozing through the openings between his fingers. "I'm settin' Patsy down, Mary Frances." He saw the frightened look on her face and added, "I've been shot before. This time won't be different."

She reached out to him to try to do something—she didn't know what—and then was thrown back against her seat as the plane started dropping. For a moment, she thought they were going to clip the twin-engine aircraft in the valley, but the plane banked, leveled out, then dropped again. She felt the plane lurch, then bounce as the aircraft touched down, then rose into the air again. They were going too fast.

The aircraft thudded onto the desert floor and began to skid hard to the right. She felt it tipping and heard a groaning sound as the left wing caught the sand and ripped away from the fuselage. As the plane plowed into the sand she thought of Josh Culhane. Why? Was she going to die? She closed her eyes and held on for life as the small plane twisted and broke up.

Suddenly the plane stopped, and she was thrown violently forward, her body wrenching against her seat belt.

She caught her breath and turned to her left.

Her hands trembled as she reached out to Charlie Tate, his head slumped over the yoke. At first his eyes were closed, but then the lids fluttered and he looked at her. "Told you these babies was easy to land," he wheezed. "Don't try—to find your way through the tunnels. You'll only get lost—lost like the Seven Cities of Cibola. Take—take the Tommy gun—" The eyes suddenly seemed to change and blood bubbled over his lips. She knew he was dead.

Mulrooney stuffed her feet into her sodden shoes and found her purse, her camera bag, her yellow rubber rain jacket.

She took the Tommy gun from Tate's lap and put it back in the guitar case, first removing the magazine, then closed the case. She pushed the case out onto the starboard wing.

At the top of her purse, she expected to find her Chiefs Special stainless. It wasn't there. She rummaged through her purse, and her right hand closed on the familiar memory-grooved stocks of the Chiefs. Culhane had given her the gun.

Slipping her camera bag and purse over her right shoulder, she threw the rain jacket ahead of her onto the wing stem and stepped out, climbing down awkwardly because of the angle of the aircraft. In her right fist she gripped the Chiefs.

The man she had seen raise his hands in the air came running over the rise.

She clamped the shiny snub-nosed revolver in both fists and swung it toward the man. "Freeze your face, asshole!" she screamed. She'd heard it in a movie once.

He stopped, then started running again, toward the plane.

She fired the revolver, and the bullet kicked up the sand two yards ahead of his feet. She'd been aiming for his upper torso, deciding the Chevrolet parked over the rise could get her to civilization as well as an aircraft with an enemy piloting it could.

The man stopped, throwing his hands into the air. "You a cop, lady?" he asked.

"I'm a lady—and that's enough with this gun in my hands. The next shot'll blow your head off!" And she lamely added, "Maybe," under her breath.

"Look, all I am is a pilot for Capezi. I don't know shit about his operations, nothin'—"

"Shut up," Mulrooney interrupted. "First I want you to take off those sunglasses. I want to see your eyes. Then you can drop your pants."

"What?" the man said as he stared at her.

"Drop your pants—and take your shoes off, too. We're going back over the rise. Reach for a gun and I'll kill you!"

Slowly he removed his dark glasses and then began to

undo his belt as he kicked out of his loafers. When he was down to his underpants and socks, Mulrooney marched him ahead of her. "What's the idea making me strip—" he called back over his shoulder.

"Can't run too far in the desert without any clothes, can you—now move it!"

When she marched him to the top of the rise, she could clearly see the thing she had noticed from the air. It was a man, hands cuffed behind his back, a sack with air holes peppering it over his head and a chain secured around his neck. His bare feet were chained about ten inches or so apart at the ankles. As she continued down the rise with her captive, the wind shifted, and she could smell the chained creature—urine, stool, sweat. When he heard their approaching sounds, the man started screaming. "Who is it—who are—"

"Go down there and let that man free—" Mulrooney ordered, turning to her prisoner.

The pilot whirled around and looked at her. "Hey, this guy's supposed to be some kind of crazy. Tried blowing up Mr. Capezi's hotel and casino up in Vegas. He's really flipped out."

"Let him go!" she shouted, gesturing with the revolver.

The pilot looked at her and started down the rise toward the bound man. "I'm tellin' you, he's crazy— drugs, the whole thing. I flew him out here."

"He's been out here a long time," Mulrooney shouted across the ten yards or so of sand. "You can smell that."

"We brought him out here maybe five, six weeks ago."

"Why did you come back—why did you come back now?"

"Mr. Capezi ordered Jess—the guy who shot at your airplane—to do it." He was working at removing the hood from the man's head; the chains were still in place.

"Why?"

The pilot ripped the hood away, falling back into the sand as the still-chained man snapped his teeth at him.

"Mr. Capezi's planning to burn down the hotel and use the kid here and his extortion note as the excuse. Some kind of trouble he's got with the organization— I don't know. Jess Adolphi talked a lot about it—shit—"

The chained man pushed to his feet. Mulrooney watched his eyes. Haltingly he started forward up the rise. "Hold it right there!" Mulrooney ordered.

The chained man kept coming, his eyes pinpoints of fiery light that terrified her.

"I'll shoot—stop!"

The chained man kept coming, his face bearded, his hair matted, his eyes squinted but penetrating into her insides. "Stop—" She fired the revolver into the sand, and the bullet buried itself eight feet in front of the still-advancing man.

She didn't think he could move too fast, but she figured that if she'd been chained with her feet a foot or so apart for weeks on end, she would have learned to hobble well, too. "Stop," she shouted again. She raised the revolver as the man's teeth snapped behind his foam-flecked lips. The pilot was making a run for it.

A shot exploded from her left, and Mulrooney threw herself to the sand. The chained man fell heavily, rolling down across the sand to the base of the rise.

Keeping her head down, Mulrooney looked to her left. The man Charlie Tate had shot with the Tommy gun was staggering across the sand from the travel trailer, his pistol raised, extended toward her. There was another gunshot, and the sand next to her erupted.

Mulrooney didn't know how far away the man was. She held the little Smith & Wesson in both hands, cocking the hammer, taking a deep breath as the man brought his pistol up to fire. Culhane had taught her some silly military word—BRASS. Breathe, Relax, Aim, Slack, Squeeze.

She did it all as fast as she could, tripping the Smith's trigger. The little gun bucked in her hands.

The man with the pistol didn't move, didn't fall. His pistol discharged into the sand less than a foot from her, and she started to cock the revolver again. The man fell over, and from the way he fell, she could somehow tell he was dead.

The pilot was running for the Chevrolet, and Mulrooney jumped to her feet and screamed after him, "I've got two shots left—want 'em?"

The pilot froze.

"On your knees!" she shouted.

He dropped and Mulrooney ran down the rise toward him, skirting the body of the chained man. She edged toward the man she had just shot, guessing he was the Jess Adolphi the pilot had spoken of. She kicked sand into his open eyes—he didn't move. She reached down with her left hand, keeping her revolver pointed at the man's head, and picked up the dead man's pistol. It was a semi-automatic and as she had never had the strength in her fingers to operate the slide on one, anyway, she threw it into the sand toward Charlie Tate's travel trailer.

She walked now toward the kneeling pilot, stopping about two or three yards short. She pointed the gun at his head. "Talk," she commanded. "If I shoot you, all I've got to do is find the keys for that black car or the pickup truck. Talk!"

The pilot looked at her, hesitated, then started to talk. "Mr. Capezi's in trouble with his father. He's been skimming the casino profits and keeping records of his take in some damn code in his computer. His father's people are breaking into the computer and could decode the program, so he's torching the hotel to get rid of the computer and cover his ass. We were supposed to fly the kid back to Vegas, drop him off and—that's it."

"Which hotel?" Mulrooney asked softly.

The pilot hesitated.

"Which hotel!" She screamed, her throat aching with the words as she shook the gun in his face.

"The Vegas Crown."

It registered. Josh was staying there. "All right, flyboy, up you get. You're taking me to Las Vegas. And before you get any ideas, just remember that two shots from the copilot's seat into the pilot's seat will be enough to finish you."

"What's to say I don't—"

Mulrooney just looked at him so he could see what she knew was written in her eyes.

"All right, all right. Will you let me go?" he asked.

"No—the police will get you."

He stood up. "What about my clothes—just my pants?"

"Never mind your clothes, just move it." She gestured with the gun. Under her breath, as he started toward the twin-engine plane, she whispered, "Like Josh says, let's see Sean Dodge top this.'

20

Josh Culhane realized it was almost pathological, competing with a creation of his own mind, but he whispered the words under his breath, anyway. "Let's see Sean Dodge top this." Then, nudging Thom Hark beside him, Culhane ran through the open door at the head of the corridor and into the main lobby, firing the F.I.E. TZ-75 pistol toward the knot of the armed invaders. He could hear Hark's Uzi chattering behind him and was glad the editor hadn't hesitated on the trigger. Culhane had seen Morrison moving restlessly on the crap table. He had listened as someone who identified himself as Mordecai Nitsch had spoken over a bullhorn to the police, who were gathered now at the front of the hotel. And he had made a decision—their only chance was to get off the main floor up into the upper levels of the building and from there organize whatever might be done against the invaders. And to do that had meant the hallway that ran from beyond the casino floor toward the stairwells and elevators to the guest floors and executive suites had to be crossed.

And the only way to accomplish that had been to make a running gunfight of it.

And Culhane ran, with Hark running beside him. Some of the invading criminals were already turning, returning submachine-gun and pistol fire. Culhane could hear Meadowshed's pistol and Dolore's subgun answering fire, as well.

Josh Culhane glanced behind him—Aaron Flaherty was down, rolling, then up, limping on his left leg, with one of the other writers helping him.

Culhane threw himself into a crouch by the elevator bank, firing the TZ-75. Hark skidded onto his knees beside him, swapping magazines in the Uzi submachine gun, then laid down a blanket of covering fire as Meadowshed and Dolore reached them. Culhane could see the others trapped in the front of one of the side rooms behind the casino floor and the mezzanine bar, heavy subgun fire pinning them down.

"Leave them," Culhane rasped. "We get out of here, they can surrender. We can't get them to the elevator banks—let the marketing man negotiate something for them. Come on," and Culhane was up, reloading the TZ-75 with a fresh magazine.

"Rather harsh to our comrades, isn't it?" Hark asked.

"It'd be harsher, Thom—a hell of a lot—if we got them killed making a run for it."

Culhane edged to the wall of elevators behind him, shouting back down the corridor to the other writers and the two publishing executives stranded behind them. "We're getting out—surrender. We'll spring you later. Don't play hero!"

He didn't wait for an answer, hearing the ding of an arriving elevator and Hark calling, "Come on—we've got one!"

"My room," Culhane shouted, running for the open elevator. Subgun fire was close now, tearing into the walls of the elevator bank. Culhane dived inside the elevator as Hark stabbed the door-close button. The echo of gunfire died on the outside of the elevator doors as Meadowshed punched the floor button. Ralph Dolore was poised at the doors with his subgun ready.

The elevator started to move, and the sounds of the gunfire became lost.

Culhane picked himself up off the floor, out of breath, and sagged against the wall of the elevator, announcing, "I've got two pistols and almost a box and a half of ammo and a Bali-Song knife in my room. We can get that stuff, then figure our next move.''

There was a lurch, and the light in the elevator flickered and went out as the elevator jolted to a stop. In the silence and the darkness, Culhane listened to the sound of the ventilation fan dying.

Then he saw the flicker of a flame—Meadowshed's lighter, his face in the yellow light almost evil looking. ''What now, friend?'' his fellow writer asked. ''Why don't you tell us what Sean Dodge would do?''

The lighter closed with an audible click, and Culhane saw the image of the lighter's flame in his eyes in the darkness. He let out a long breath and said, ''The ceilings aren't too high in the guest rooms—can't be much between floors. If there's a trapdoor on top, we go out through it. If there isn't—''

''I know—we'll be trapped.'' It was Thom Hark's voice, tinged with a mixture of panic and laughter. ''I've always been a quick study.''

''Nope,'' Culhane said in response. ''We just use one of the subguns like a can opener and cut a hole in the top of the elevator. Somebody get down and give me a boost, and I'll check for a trapdoor.''

''May as well be me—what the hell,'' said a voice. Culhane recognized it as Meadowshed's.

21

Lew Wilson and an FDLE SWAT team had arrived at the house less than five minutes after the local police— Dan Track had appreciated the opportunity to lower his hands. After the telephone lines had been cut during the conversation with Sir Abner Chesterton, Chesterton had called Wilson and Wilson had called the local police. Track sat now on one of the swivel chairs of the Consortium's chartered business jet. Wilson and George were seated in chairs opposite him at the small but ample round table between them.

Five minutes after Wilson had arrived, a call had come in on Wilson's radio from Chesterton. The Vegas Crown hotel-and-casino complex in Las Vegas had been taken over by a group of heavily armed commandos led by a man named Mordecai Nitsch. The casino was owned by associates of Crazy Carlo Capezi and managed by Capezi's only surviving offspring, Joe. Mordecai Nitsch was a known member of the émigré mob called the Malina. The Vegas Crown was insured by a Consortium member company.

"Vengeance against the Capezi family—maybe that's it," Lew Wilson volunteered, breaking the silence. "Rob them blind of casino profits. The Las Vegas police think there was some sort of shooting incident right at the beginning of the robbery. Some people were just entering the casino when the shooting started and ran for it. Maybe it made the plan go sour and that's why it's turned into a hostage situation."

"You think Nitsch would really blow up the whole hotel and everybody in it?" George asked.

Track found himself smiling, saying to his nephew, "Sometimes you have a decided advantage in world outlook being in your middle twenties. If you were Nitsch, surrounded by cops, the National Guard moving in, and you had a few dozen confederates with you and they were all very likely members of the Malina just like you, what would you do? Turn yourself in for a couple of consecutive life sentences and maybe get back on the street when you turned eighty, or risk it all?"

George didn't answer.

"Sir Abner and Colonel Gorzinski, the Israeli security specialist he mentioned, should be in Las Vegas a half-hour ahead of us—time enough to coordinate with the local law, maybe get a rundown on this Nitsch character, see what the hell he's made of," Wilson announced.

"I'll bet it's not rats and snails and puppy dogs' tails," said Track as he snapped down the guillotine to cut off the tip of one of his cigars.

22

There had been a trapdoor leading from the top of the elevator, and Culhane had gone through first. Behind him came Thom Hark, followed by Meadowshed and Dolore. Getting another boost from Bob Meadowshed, Culhane felt in the darkness above for the elevator doorframe opening on the next floor. There was little time. If the invaders of the Vegas Crown had been able to shut down the elevator so quickly, he had little doubt they could determine where the elevator had stopped, and then it was only a matter of time before men would be on their trail.

"Get me up a little higher," Culhane coaxed.

"I thought this was supposed to be a writers' conference, not a gymnastics class," Meadowshed groused from the darkness below him.

"That's just another fringe benefit of working for us," Hark quipped. "You see, we realize what a horribly sedentary life the typical writer must lead. This is all a clever ploy to heighten our writers' physical fitness."

Dolore made one of his rare comments, "Fuck off."

"Charming thought, but hardly the place and hardly the company," Hark countered.

"All right, guys," Culhane growled as his fingers found the crack between the two doors. "Anybody got a knife? I need something to pry with."

"Wait a minute—" said Meadowshed. "Watch out, it's sharp. And try not to break it."

Culhane felt the body-heated metal in his left hand as

he reached down into the darkness. His fist closed on the skeletonized handle of a Russell Sting knife, and he inserted it in the crack between the doors. "A.G. makes strong knives," Culhane groaned, starting to pry, "but somehow I don't think he meant them to be used like this!" he exclaimed.

Culhane forced the doors apart two inches, enough room to get his fingers into the opening and pry them farther apart. A pale shaft of light from the hallway poked through the doors, and he lowered the knife down to Meadowshed.

Culhane settled his body against the side of the elevator shaft, both hands in the crack between the shaft doors, and pushed. The doors were almost impossible to move. "I know who installed these," Culhane grunted. "Conan the Barbarian. Jeez, where's Superman when you really need him?" He realized he was making noises like a midget trying to defecate a bowling ball, but the doors were moving. Culhane was able to push his right arm between the doors, using his upper arm as a brace against the right-hand door, pushing at the left-side door with his hands. The doors moved. The increased light almost blinded him. He bent forward, getting both forearms and then both upper arms through the opening, putting his shoulder muscles to work. The doors split back from him, and Culhane clawed at the carpeted floor, squinting against the light, twisting his body, nearly losing the TZ-75.

And then he was through, rolling onto his back. From his left he heard a sound, and rolling onto his side, he gripped the TZ-75 in his right fist. There was no time to raise the gun into a proper firing position, and with the left side of the frame and slide parallel to the carpeted floor, Culhane jerked the trigger as the submachine-gun-armed invader raised his Uzi to fire.

Culhane's pistol fired first, and two splotches of red blossomed on the cloth shirt just over his assailant's sternum. The subgunner dropped, his Uzi never firing.

Culhane came to his feet, and Thom Hark emerged from the darkness of the elevator shaft. "What the hell was that?" he asked, looking down the hall at the fallen gunner.

"I think he was just a straggler, but if there are a bunch of them up here, we'll know in a second or so. Get over there and get his guns. I'll help Meadowshed and Dolore out of the shaft."

Hark was on his feet. The Uzi came to a natural assault position as he advanced on the dead subgunner.

Culhane leaned toward the shaft. "One of you guys—come on—" As he grabbed for a set of hands in the darkness of the shaft, he snapped, "Thom—what the hell floor are we on?"

"Eighth—yes, eighth."

"My floor—we're in luck. I just hope it isn't bad luck."

Culhane put his back into his work, and Meadowshed crawled through, stepping from Ralph Dolore's back.

"Take the other end of the corridor, Bob, and send Thom down to the right. Watch for bad guys."

"Right." Meadowshed nodded grimly, his blond hair fallen over the left side of his forehead.

Culhane reached down into the darkness. "I'm edgin' closer, Ralph—reach for me." Culhane balanced on the edge of the shaft on his waist, his legs splayed to keep his balance and keep himself from inadvertently being pulled down into the shaft. He could feel Dolore's fingers as his own fingers moved down through the palm of the man's hand, wrapping tightly around the right wrist.

He looked toward Dolore, seeing the oddly quiet writer bracing against the shaft wall, moving steadily upward. Culhane tried shifting his weight back, but couldn't; his arms ached. He pulled hard, and suddenly Dolore was up, falling across him through the opening, then rolling off as Culhane felt the weight go.

"Give me a hand with the doors—I want to shut them if we can. Let the guys guess where we came out if they don't already know from monitoring the elevator. Then we can move the body of the guy I croaked," and Culhane set his weight to the right-side door with Dolore on the left one. The doors began to close. "Hey, wait a minute. I've got a better idea," Culhane announced.

Culhane ran to the body of the dead man. Hark had already stripped the body of weapons, even turning out the linings of the pockets. Culhane grabbed the dead man by the ankles, dragging him—for once he was happy all the carpets in the place were red since the carpeting would hide the bloodstains. "Give me a hand dropping our friend here," Culhane said as he dragged the body nearer to the open elevator doors. With Dolore's help, Culhane stuffed the body through the opening and let it drop. "So long," Culhane said as he got to his feet, throwing his weight to the door again, with Dolore doing the same. Culhane grunted and pushed, and the doors shifted slowly until at last they closed.

Culhane sagged back against the wall, taking a deep breath, summoning back his *chi*, drawing to him all his strength. He stood up, away from the wall. "Let's go, Ralph. You get Thom and Meadowshed, and I'll head for my room—814." Culhane started running, the TZ-75, hammer down, safety off, in his right fist. He looked down at his clothes, grease stained from the elevator shaft, his hands the same way.

He reached 814, stopped, put his key in the lock, twisted fast and stepped away.

There was no gunfire from inside, no flurry of movement.

Culhane rolled through the doorway—a dumb thing to do in reality, he knew, but no worse than any other manner for one man to enter a room where there might be an armed enemy. There was none.

Culhane stood up and moved to the closet, taking out

his suitcase. He wiped his grease-covered hands on the sides of his Levi's and opened the case, nudging aside his clothes with the backs of his wrists. The Scoremaster was still in its case, as was the Detonics Combat Master.

Detecting movement, Culhane wheeled toward the doorway—it was Hark, Meadowshed and Dolore. Stepping back, he surveyed their arsenal—three subguns, five pistols and an assortment of knives. They had a chance, however slight it was.

But a chance to do what?

Thom Hark said it, and Culhane tried to laugh but couldn't. "I have no fear," Hark said. "You are three of the greatest action-adventure writers in the world. It should be a mere nothing with your combined mental powers for you to concoct a plot that wipes out these terrorists, or whatever they are, sets free all the hostage patrons, makes us all look splendidly heroic and still gets us out of this alive."

Dolore made one of his rare remarks.

"Sure."

23

The sick feeling in his stomach wasn't from the pain-killer the doctor had given him. It was from the realization that it had all gone wrong and from the knowledge that only he could make it right. With one man on each side of him carrying the chair his smashed leg confined him to, Nitsch had himself moved forward to the four-story-high glass front of the Vegas Crown. The rank of ten chosen hostages cowered just ahead of him as a shield against possible police or National Guard gun-fire. The other hostages were being held in the casino.

"Set me down here," he ordered his two followers. He raised the bullhorn and squeezed the handle so it would carry his voice, amplify it. "This is Mordecai Nitsch," he announced through the open doors. The air conditioning was a rush of cold behind him. "If there is any attempt to interfere with me, these ten hostages will die first. The hundreds of others inside will die immediately afterward. I have the hotel mined with explosives—if you doubt me, I am utilizing more than three hundred pounds of your own favorite military explosive, C-4. It is enough to level this hotel and almost totally destroy buildings on both sides and across the street. I have a list of demands. They must be carried out to the letter, or all here will die. If they are carried out to the letter, after my men and I, accompanied by a number of hostages, have made good our escape, you will be duly notified as to how to defuse the explosives and, of course, their locations.

"In two hours, the following must be accomplished.

It is not impossible. No time extensions will be granted. First, one hundred million dollars shall be brought to me by a manner I shall detail later. It shall be in unmarked American currency, in denominations not exceeding twenty dollars. When the money is brought, I will require radiation testing equipment, an infrared scanner and a modest supply of common chemicals that I will delineate at the time the money is to be delivered, all, of course, to test the money for markings.

"Second," Nitsch continued, "I'll require a sufficient number of buses to accommodate my five dozen men and an equal number of hostages. Third, two 747 jet aircraft fueled and ready at the airport, crew to consist of two overseas-rated pilots for each craft, each craft to be equipped with necessary charts for travel from here to any part of the world." He looked at the Omega on his left wrist. "You have exactly two hours. After two hours, should my demands not have been met, all here will die and this building will be totally destroyed."

Nitsch had planned it differently. Escape with the casino proceeds had been the game—so far the money netted from the casino vaults was in excess of three-and-one-half million dollars. Then, blow the hotel, leaving Moishe Sebin's body to be found with the incriminating documents.

Now his primary concern was not to serve the KGB or to frame the government of Israel for an act of revenge on American soil. His primary concern was to live.

He spoke through the bullhorn again. "Some of you may suppose I could not bring myself to kill all the so-called innocent people in this fine hotel. To reassure you that I am wholly capable of such an act, I offer the following demonstration. One of these ten hostages will be killed as an example."

He watched, not really enjoying it as the ten hostages turned, looking back toward him, some of them starting to speak. He took his pistol, selected one at random—a woman in her thirties, or so—and shot her three times in the spinal cord.

The body slumped to the concrete steps just in front of the open doors.

He looked to his two chair bearers. "Carry me inside," he commanded. "Then order the other hostages back. Leave the body of the dead woman, but do not allow the police to retrieve it. It will serve as a reminder."

Mordecai Nitsch looked away from the woman as they picked up his chair and turned it around to carry him inside.

THROUGH THE OPEN GLASS DOORS to the small balcony off his room, Culhane heard the reverberating voice of the leader of the terrorists and recognized it as the voice that belonged to the desert warrior—a man who called himself Mordecai Nitsch. As he changed out of his grease-stained clothes, he listened to Nitsch's demands, then heard the three shots. Had a hostage really been murdered? He glanced at the luminous black face of his Rolex Sea-Dweller. The police and military had until six-fifteen in the evening to produce the money, the buses and the airplanes for Nitsch and his men to escape.

Culhane walked toward the balcony, threading the Milt Sparks BN-55 cross-draw holster to his belt, then threading the belt through the rest of the loops.

Standing on the balcony were Thom Hark, Bob Meadowshed and the taciturn but efficient Ralph Dolore. "Any brilliant plans yet?" Culhane asked.

The sunlight on the balcony was bright. Overhead, Culhane could see military helicopters circling the building. But there was no way to signal them, short of taking a shot at them. He had tried his room phone—the switchboard was out.

There was no immediate answer from either of his

two fellow adventure writers or the editorial director he and the other two writers shared.

Culhane turned away from the balcony and walked over to the bed. He picked up the stainless-steel Detonics Scoremaster .45, dumping the magazine, working the slide. He locked the slide back, upping the slide stop. He replaced the 7-round Detonics magazine, seating it, then working down the slide stop, chambering the top round. He upped the ambidextrous thumb safety, leaving the pistol cocked and locked, and holstered it in the Sparks cross-draw rig.

"You seem to thrive on devious plots." It was Thom Hark's voice.

Culhane didn't answer for a moment. He began to check the little Detonics Combat Master stainless, his second .45. He repeated the process with the magazine, opening the slide, visually inspecting the pistol. He replaced the loaded magazine after giving the spine a solid whack into the palm of his left hand.

He replaced the magazine, worked down the slide stop. This time he lowered the hammer, slowly and carefully. He inserted it into the Alessi shoulder rig on the bed, closing the speed-break snap through the trigger guard. Two spare magazines hung vertically from the offside portion of the harness. He started to pull the shoulder rig on. "The way I see it, we can't stay here. Maybe we could stay here and hide, but we can't stay here and be of any use in stopping these suckers. So, we can either go up to the roof or down toward the first floor. On the roof I don't know what we'd find. On the first floor I know what we'll find. We can't communicate with the authorities. The only phones that should still work are pay phones—they wouldn't run off the switchboard. But the only pay phones are on the first floor, as far as I know. Same with the phones in the privately owned shops in the mall behind the casino and off to the side of the pool. But we can't get to those phones, either, without crossing the main floor. Anyway, cops would just tell us to do something dumb, like hide out or surrender to the terrorists.''

''So we go down.'' Meadowshed nodded.

''Yeah—because they won't expect that. They won't know for sure we're better armed than we were earlier. They don't really know anything about us. I doubt if they took the time to match the registration cards from the front desk with the people they hold hostage downstairs.''

''What about the hotel guests who weren't downstairs or out of the building?'' Hark asked.

Culhane looked at Hark. ''Probably hiding in their rooms or the stairwells. Some of them might be asleep and not even know about it.''

''We could put together a small army, then.'' Hark smiled.

''An army of people we don't have enough weapons for and who don't know what they're doing would just get in the way. All we'd do is precipitate a bloodbath,'' Culhane responded.

''Just the four of us, then,'' Meadowshed murmured.

Culhane settled the shoulder rig, the holster with the little Detonics snugged under his left armpit.

Ralph Dolore spoke. ''Four of us against all of them is crazy.''

Culhane looked at him. ''That Mordecai Nitsch character said he'd planted explosives. He said he'd bring this hotel down. Now in Takers number seven—''

''Shut up about your damn Sean Dodge,'' Dolore shouted, turning his back and walking to the balcony.

''Explosives.'' Hark nodded, raising his eyebrows, a conspiratorial smile lighting his face.

''Explosives. I got together with a good friend of mine who'd done OSS and clandestine work. He was blowing things up in both theaters of operation during World War Two, and lots of other places afterward.

He's a genius with the stuff. He taught me how to play with plastic explosives, even let me blow up a few things, and then he taught me how to disarm the charges. Some of them can't be disarmed, but we'll have to gamble these can be. If we knock out their ability to blow the place up, then wait until they abandon most of the hostages to board their buses, we might have a chance of turning the tables on them when they try to reach the buses. Even if we can't, at least we'll have prevented them from detonating the explosives and save several hundred lives. It's worth a try. Best plot I can think of,'' and he felt himself smiling. "After all, I didn't outline this one, the characters aren't mine—I've got lots of excuses."

Thom Hark—Culhane guessed because it was his job to review plots and determine their viability—looked to Meadowshed and Dolore, who had turned back from the balcony. "Any better ideas, any amendments, additions?"

"Only one," Meadowshed said after a moment. "If we work our way down to search for their explosives, we'll cover more territory and reduce the risk of all of us getting caught up in a one-way firefight if we split into two teams."

Dolore spoke. "If we assume that the bulk of the enemy force is below us, with the exception of some stragglers and maybe some industrious looters, then we should give one team a two-minute head start down each stairwell as we take it. If the first team gets into a little trouble, it'll give the second team time to prepare to counter it without just falling into it. And if the first team gets into more trouble than combined we can successfully handle, it'll give the second team a chance to back away, take another route and continue the operation."

"Agreed." Culhane nodded. He checked the Pacific Cutlery Bali-Song on his belt, giving it a good-luck fast opening. "You and Meadowshed are the backup team," he said to Dolore. "You'll have one subgun apiece. Make sure Thom here has a pistol to go along with his subgun."

Meadowshed crossed to the bed, picking up a Beretta 92SB taken from the man Culhane had shot after exiting the elevator shaft. "Perfect gun for you, Thom—the Beretta here."

Culhane looked at Hark, Meadowshed and Dolore. He gestured toward the bathroom. "Anybody have to pee before we get started?"

Meadowshed just stabbed two pistols into his belt, took spare magazines, then picked up an Uzi and started for the door opening on the hallway.

JOE CAPEZI HAD SET THE DETONATORS. Angry, he looked at his wristwatch under the gray light cast by the overhead fluorescent fixtures on the landing above. If he had realized that at some point between the time he reached the subbasement and the time he completed doing what he had to do the elevators would shut down and he would be forced to hike the stairwells to the top floor and his helicopter, he would have delayed the timing mechanisms.

The plastic explosives had been purchased on the L.A. black market. The quartz-crystal oscillator chips and the other electronic parts had been purchased in a variety of radio-supply stores throughout the southwest. The painter's-grade aluminum powder had been purchased in Denver. The fertilizer—high in ammonium nitrate—had been purchased in Cheyenne, Wyoming.

Jess Adolphi had purchased the explosives, while Milton had gathered the electronic components. Capezi himself had bought the ammonium nitrate fertilizer. The painter's-grade aluminum powder had been purchased by phone and shipped to a blind address in Santa Fe, New Mexico.

One man had coordinated the effort, and he was dead. Capezi reflected that he was probably better off for it. Through the services of a woman who had worked for a San Francisco VA hospital, an explosives expert with a classified military background had been found. The woman had been killed by Jess Adolphi, the murder made to look like a street mugging gone bad. The veteran, partially addicted to painkillers as a result of wounds sustained in Vietnam, had been kidnapped, addicted to heroin, then let out cold. To feed his monkey, he had to cooperate and build highly effective incendiary devices. Adolphi had murdered him when they had secured and prepared the devices, testing a much smaller version in the desert. The body had been dropped from a boat somewhere off the California coast.

Joe Capezi stopped for a moment to catch his breath. Ten floors still remained. The stairs were hard, steep, the atmosphere confining.

He got his breathing to a more regular rate, more through concentration than anything else, and continued up the stairs. In one hour, the detonators would activate and the hotel would be a twenty-eight-story torch.

24

Dan Track, with George and Lew Wilson flanking him, peered through the borrowed Aimpoint black-armored dualfocus 8X30s at the Vegas Crown complex across the street. "Oh, boy," he groaned. "How many stories, Sir Abner? I stopped counting at twenty."

Sir Abner Chesterton, with the Israeli U.N. aide, Zbigniew Gorzinski beside him, answered, "Twenty-eight, Dan."

Track looked at Chesterton, then at Gorzinski. The Israeli had "professional" written all over him in capital letters. Track guessed he was Mossad. "In the past hour, just after Colonel Gorzinski and I arrived from New York," Chesterton began, "the helicopters circling the hotel have indicated at least a dozen of the Malina terrorists have come onto the roof. There is a helicopter there belonging to the hotel. Joe Capezi is a licensed helicopter pilot, but there's been no sign of Capezi, and according to Colonel Gorzinski, Mordecai Nitsch is not helicopter qualified. Took three or four lessons in single-engine aircraft and gave up."

"What color socks does he prefer?" Track asked Gorzinski, not laughing.

"Olive drab—when he's working," Gorzinski responded emotionlessly.

Track looked around. Local police, state police and National Guard personnel were everywhere. "Sir Abner, is there someplace private where the five of us could talk?"

"The car I rented at the airport."

"Fine." Track nodded. "Lead the way."

Sir Abner Chesterton started ahead, weaving through the crowd, Track behind him, Gorzinski behind Track, George and Lew Wilson bringing up the rear. It took several minutes to reach the adjoining street that formed a right angle with the broad thoroughfare that the Vegas Crown fronted. There were police barricades at the far end of the street. Sir Abner walked into the street and toward a white Ford four-door sedan.

He stopped at the driver's-side door, fumbled the keys and opened it, then reached inside to get the back-door button. He slid behind the wheel, leaned across and got the front-and-rear passenger-side door locks. The front passenger door popped open as Dan Track crossed around the hood of the car. Track climbed in beside Chesterton, while George got into the back beside Wilson and the Israeli.

Dan Track looked forward through the windshield and said to Chesterton, "How much longer until we reach the deadline?"

"Six-fifteen, local time," Chesterton replied.

Track nodded, glancing at his watch. "About an hour. You say they said they're using C-4?"

"Yes, why?"

"Just thinking how I'd blow up a building like that if I were these guys." Track looked down the street. He could see most of the Vegas Crown. He turned around in his seat, unzipping the front of his brown leather bomber jacket, looking at the Israeli. "Colonel Gorzinski, you're going to have to level with me. Mossad or ex-Mossad?"

The Israeli—tall, lean, deeply tanned, a high forehead and thinning hair, piercing blue eyes—stared directly at Track.

"Well?"

"I am not 'ex,' " he admitted, grinning.

Chesterton interrupted. "Colonel Gorzinski is ostensibly attached to the U.N., but he's really here working with the FBI out of New York, where Malina activity is very high. He is Deputy Director for Covert Operations for the Mossad.'' Chesterton turned around in his seat, leaning his left forearm on the steering wheel, his right on the seat back. ''I'm sorry, Colonel, there was never any need to conceal your identity from Major Track, and now it's rather vital that he knows it.''

Lew Wilson spoke, pushing his glasses up from the bridge of his nose a little as he did. ''They finally got something solid on a Malina-KGB connection, huh?''

Gorzinski said, ''There is no connection that can be proved, but it appears extremely likely that the KGB controls the Malina. This particular Malina operation may be what we have waited for. For a considerable period of time, we have suspected a major act of terrorism to be perpetrated on your shores by the Malina, then used by Soviet propagandists to generate anti-Israeli, even anti-Semitic sentiment in the United States.''

''Most of these guys are Russians, right?'' Wilson asked.

Gorzinski nodded. ''Yes, but many of them—not all, mind you, but many—emigrated from Russia to Israel, spent some time in our state, then left for other parts of the world, among them the United States. Those who did spend time in Israel in many cases served in the Israeli military, in a few cases in Israeli intelligence.'' He shrugged broadly. ''We were duped. In your country, you might well call it being a good Christian to help one's fellow man, to trust. We called it, albeit subconsciously, being a good Jew. We endeavored, through various organizations operating in Europe and in your own United States, to do all that was humanly possible to help these victims of anti-Semitic oppression inside the Soviet Union. In some cases, they came to us with valuable skills that could well be utilized in intelligence work. Criminals sometimes make able agents.''

"George used to be in intelligence work," Chesterton volunteered.

"Thanks a lot," George said defensively. "In my outfit, if somebody got a traffic ticket he could lose his clearance."

"The work we sometimes engage in is somewhat different from the activities in your background." Gorzinski smiled. "You see, Sir Abner allowed that I read your file, and yours," and he turned to Dan Track. Then he looked at Wilson. "I'm afraid Sir Abner had no file data on you, Agent Wilson, but he spoke highly of your abilities and your long-standing friendship with Major Track."

"What kind of training do these guys have?" Track interjected.

"I have no idea what those relative few who are active KGB have been exposed to, but I should say all levels of field-agent indoctrination, all the latest material in clandestine work behind enemy lines, sabotage, assassination, infiltration," Gorzinski answered.

"Wonderful," Track said, suddenly feeling warm in the car. He rolled down his window, then pulled out one of his cigars and his Zippo. He guillotined the cigar, then lit the dark tobacco.

Gorzinski said, "It is safe to assume that at least one of the men inside the hotel, likely this Mordecai Nitsch, whom we have been interested in interviewing for some time now, has the very best training the KGB can offer. And as you know, an objective ranking of world intelligence-gathering agencies places Mossad as number one, KGB as number two and your own CIA as number three. Nitsch has the benefit of the expertise of both number two and number one."

"Just like working days for Hertz and nights for Avis—wonderful," Track said, inhaling the cigar smoke.

"The ransom is being gathered," Chesterton put in.

"Actually, one hundred million dollars in small unmarked bills isn't that difficult to obtain in Las Vegas. I understand Don Carlo Capezi is en route to Las Vegas—his son, of course, is trapped inside the Vegas Crown."

"Great. What's Capezi going to do—storm the place with a Thompson submachine gun?" Track didn't expect an answer, and added, "Okay—I've got to get in there. Will the local police cooperate?"

"The FBI has all but ordered them to," Chesterton answered. "After your success against Johannes Krieger, it helps to have friends like the ones you made."

"They couldn't have smuggled tons of C-4 in," Track said, thinking out loud. "So with only a little—three hundred pounds you told me—what could they do?" He turned around again, looking at Zbigniew Gorzinski. "You're in the same business, but on the other side of the coin. What would you do if you wanted to bring down a twenty-eight-story hotel?"

Gorzinski seemed lost in thought for a moment. "Well, I should say—and of course this is purely hypothetical, purely speculative—"

"Oh, yeah," Track said, "I knew it would be speculative, but lay it on me, anyway."

"The most economical and surely successful system, provided sandbags were available—"

"There was construction on the south wing. Would bags of concrete suffice?"

Gorzinski looked at Chesterton. "Yes, admirably so."

"You mean, whack out the support columns on one side of the building and topple the hotel like a tree under a chain saw," Track said.

"Precisely." Gorzinski nodded to Track, sighing loudly.

"Third floor or second?" Track asked.

"Again, purely speculative."

"Cut out with the 'speculative,' huh?"

"All right. If I were doing it, considering the construction, I'd go for the third floor. The rooms could have been rented out in advance, the plastique and the detonators put in place, all of that overnight. Then after the takeover, simply wire the detonators to work when required and stem the charges properly with the cement bags."

Track exhaled a cloud of gray smoke, aiming it for the open window. "I've got to get in there," he said again. "Take out the explosives, then see what can be done on the hostage situation. Otherwise—" and he looked at Chesterton "—otherwise they'll walk right out of here, board their little damn airplanes and wind up somewhere like Albania, right?"

"Yes, and likely leave behind some rather incriminating false evidence against the Israeli people. I should say that's the root motive for the entire operation," Gorzinski added.

"Gotcha," Track said. He looked at Chesterton. "Then the FBI and the local people will let me do what I want?"

"With the reservation that at the same time they will be collecting the ransom and that no local police can be involved—simply so they can disavow your actions to the Malina should your operation be lacking in success. A hedge against the Malina killing more hostages," Chesterton said.

From where he sat, Track could see the body of the woman outside the four-story glass front of the Vegas Crown. He didn't know her name, nor did the police, nor likely did Mordecai Nitsch when he shot her. Her death only reinforced for him his belief that there were people in the world who couldn't be allowed to do what they did, who needed to be stopped in whatever way was available, by whatever means.

No one had appointed him God, given him the right to determine who lived and who died. But despite joking about it over the years, he was fully aware of his abilities and gifts. And aware, too, that but for the love and concern of the sister who had raised him; the Chicago judge who had urged him to join the Army; his first sergeant who had looked into him and seen something better, then all but threatened him with dismemberment if he didn't pursue schooling—but for all these people, he could easily have been a Johannes Krieger, a Mordecai Nitsch, or perhaps someone more terrible than either. He thought of something his sister had once said—no one is more zealous than the convert. He had had his vacation from responsibility.

He turned away from the woman's body, whispering, "God bless you, lady," and looked at George and Lew Wilson. "Nobody has to come along—" he began.

"Naw, nobody has to." George smiled. "But I will, anyway."

"I didn't fly all the way from Miami to Las Vegas just to sit around," Lew Wilson said.

Track worked the handle, swinging open the Ford's passenger door, stepped out and almost knocked down a pretty but frantic-looking girl running toward the car. Two Las Vegas policemen were trying to catch up with her. She had auburn hair falling past her shoulders and large hazel-green eyes. She was about five-seven, Track guessed—without the mud-stained white track shoes she wore. Her pink long-sleeved T-shirt was dirt stained. Her Levi's had seen better days, as well. And there was one of the largest leather shoulder bags, dark maroon in color, that he had ever come across, hanging from the right side of her body.

He couldn't help feeling he had seen her somewhere before.

Breathless, she leaned against the car, saying, "Are you Major Track?"

"Dan Track—I haven't been a major for a while. The rank just sort of sticks to me no matter how much I try to discourage it."

"Good for you," she answered dismissively. "I'm M.F. Mulrooney."

"Hey, I knew I'd seen you before. I've read some of your books. When's *Occult Murmurs* coming out?"

"Real soon—I'll send you an autographed copy. Listen, there's a bomb—a couple of bombs—inside the Vegas Crown!" Mulrooney said, her voice betraying her agitation.

"I know," Track replied coolly.

"You know?" Mulrooney shouted. "Then what the hell are you doing about it? And what's all this stuff I've heard about some gang of Israeli terrorists taking over the hotel?"

"They're not all Israelis," Track said, still cool. "Turns out most of them are Russian originally. It's a gang called the Malina, and we know they have the hotel mined with explosives. We're taking steps—"

"I don't give a shit what steps you're taking," Mulrooney exploded. "Just do something!"

"Yeah," Track said to her, getting a little angry, biting down hard on his cigar. She was fumbling in her purse, pulled out a package of Salems.

He lit the cigarette for her with his Zippo and said, "Why don't you tell me what you know?"

"This old man, a really nice old guy named Charlie Tate, who used to fly with Chennault and the Flying Tigers—anyway, he found the Seven Golden Cities of Cibola two years ago in the Nevada desert and was going to take me to them. But some gangsters who worked for Joe Capezi had this man at Charlie's place in the desert who threatened to blow up the Vegas Crown or burn it down, or something, and the pilot—"

"The guy who flew with Chennault?"

"No, the guy who flew the Beechcraft with Jess Adolphi—"

"Who the hell is Jess Adolphi?"

"He helped Capezi make the firebombs to destroy the hotel—"

"What firebombs?"

"The ones in the elevator shafts—to destroy the computer—"

"Computer?"

"The one Capezi used to embezzle the thirteen million dollars that the mob found out about. That's why he had to burn down the hotel. And he was going to do it today!"

"But he can't do it today," Track said. "The other guys in there, the Malina, they're going to blow up the hotel—"

"But Josh Culhane is in there, damn you, and I love him even if he does run around the world trying to live out all his adventures before he puts them into his damn-crazy adventure novels, and the local police said you were pretty much in charge of whatever could be done to stop what's going on in the hotel and I should ask you to save Josh—and Joe Capezi's going to burn it down and you say these other guys are going to blow it up and—aw, shit," and suddenly she was gone.

Track looked down—she'd sat down on the curbstone so abruptly he'd momentarily lost her. Track dropped into a crouch beside her, noticing Wilson, George, Sir Abner Chesterton and Zbigniew Gorzinski form a semicircle around them.

"He was supposed to meet me," she sniffed. "And the old man died—"

"The one who flew with Chennault?"

"Yeah. He got killed when we were in the desert and this crazy drug addict in chains tried biting me to death until Adolphi killed him. Then I shot Adolphi and I made the pilot fly me back here without his pants, and we called the police on the radio, and Joe Capezi's going to burn down his hotel with these big firebombs with plastique and gasoline and some other stuff I can't remember—"

Track looked up at Gorzinski.

Gorzinski volunteered, "Painter's-grade aluminum powder?"

"Yeah, I think so," she said as she looked up, sniffing loudly, her cheeks tear streaked. "Who the hell are you?"

"He's with Israeli intelligence," Lew Wilson offered.

"So who are you?" she asked Wilson.

"He's with the Florida Department of Law Enforcement," Chesterton told her.

"And who are *you*?" she asked.

"I represent a cartel of the world's largest insurance underwriters called the Consortium. We insure the Vegas Crown."

"Oh, and who's he?" she said, looking at Track's nephew.

"He's just George," Track said. "How many bombs does Capezi have?"

"One in each elevator shaft. Why?"

"Holy shit—sorry," and he looked away from her.

"Yeah, you be sorry. I'm already sorry. If Culhane gets himself killed—aw, shit, I don't know—and the old man in the desert—"

Track stood up, looked at Wilson, George, Chesterton and Gorzinski. "Sir Abner, you mind the store. Gorzinski, you get a group of people ready to come in and back us up when we find the explosives and neutralize them. And while we get ready, find this crazy pilot she's talking about—"

"The one who flew with Chennault?" Gorzinski asked.

"No, the one without his pants. Get more information on the firebombs." Track turned to Wilson and George. "Let's get our gear."

"What gear, I didn't bring any gear," Wilson said.

"My uncle's got enough for everybody," George told him.

Track turned to M.F. Mulrooney. "Hey, listen, Miss Mulrooney."

"You can call me Mary Frances—or M.F., if you like."

"Okay, Mary Frances. Look, we'll try to get in there, maybe try to find Culhane—wait a minute, do you mean Josh Culhane, the guy who writes The Takers?"

"Yeah, that's the guy."

Track nodded. "I'm a big fan of his, so don't worry, okay?" he said.

She looked up at him, still sitting on the curbstone like a forlorn puppy. " 'Don't worry'—sure. Look, if it's all the same with you, I'll worry for a little while longer, okay?"

Track just walked away, George and Lew Wilson beside him.

25

Dan Track rolled from the rack welded under the frame of the bus, hitting the street harder than he'd wanted to, and moved toward the hedgerow on the far side of the Vegas Crown, flattening himself to the sandy ground beside the shrubbery. George followed him out of the rack, clawing his way to a crouch, then running to the hedgerow and positioning himself behind Dan Track. Track watched Wilson do the same as the bus turned the corner, with Wilson rolling toward the curb, then taking a position beside George.

Track rasped, "I don't think they saw us." The sirens from the additional police vehicles Track had ordered brought in to the other side of the hotel should have attracted their attention, Track hoped.

"We ready?" George asked.

"Hell, I'm ready," Wilson said.

Track remained silent as he studied the roofline and reflected on this task ahead of him—a commando operation in broad daylight. The Malina bombs were set to blow in forty-five minutes. There was perhaps less time before Capezi's firebombs were set off. The mission had insanity, suicide and plain stupidity written all over it, he thought. Maybe that's why he was doing it.

"Let's go," and he was up, running the length of the hedgerow in a low crouch, the SPAS-12 on its sling, cross body from his left shoulder, the pistol grip in his gloved right fist, the front hand guard in his left. Under his left armpit was the Metalife Custom L-Frame. At his right kidney, the Trapper Scorpion .45. Strapped to his left calf was a Gerber MkII fighting knife. The back of each of his leather gloves was fitted with three tiny integral sheaths, each sheath carrying a stainless-steel *shuriken* throwing spike. Hanging from his left shoulder, cross-body to his right side, was an olive-drab GI map-and-photo case that he used like a musette bag, containing spare shells for the SPAS, Detonics 8-round extension magazines for the Trapper Scorpion, Safariland speedloaders for the L-Frame and two Eggs—sound-and-light grenades. On his left side, cross-body from his right shoulder, was a gas-mask bag. The front of his battered brown leather bomber jacket was zipped halfway up, the patch pockets bulging with spare rounds for the SPAS. He had been offered body armor by the police, but he didn't like armor—it slowed him down and its promise of protection made him more reckless than he liked.

Reaching the side of the hotel, Track flattened himself against a concrete support post, waiting for George and Wilson to reach the wall of the building. Both George and Wilson carried musette bags, gas masks and M-16s. Slung tight across George's chest was a Walther MKP 9mm subgun, while Wilson had elected to carry a Beretta 92SB. Track had insisted that all three carry silencer-fitted Walther P-5 9mms, as well, to deal with guards at the basement doorway.

George slammed into the wall beside Track, breathless, thumbing his black Jack Daniels baseball cap up from his forehead. Sweat beaded on his upper lip over the pencil-thin black mustache he wore. "I would have never made an infantryman," he said as he grinned at Track.

Wilson joined them, adjusting the elastic strap that held his glasses in place. "Where to?" he panted.

"Around to the basement. We know when the Malina explosives are set to go," Track said as he rolled back the cuff of his bomber jacket and checked his watch.

"Another forty minutes. But we don't know when Capezi's fireworks start, so we've got to take them out first."

"You sure this deal is going to work?" George asked. "I've never heard of using C-4 for anything else but blowing things up."

Track grinned broadly. "You can count on me, George. Would I lead you into a no-win situation?"

"Why did you ask me that?"

Track laughed, then started to run the perimeter of the building. When he thought about this for an instant, he decided it might make a good epitaph—"He kept running—hard." But he hoped he wouldn't be needing an epitaph too soon.

JOSH CULHANE HEARD TELLTALE sounds of other human beings in the stairwell below. He turned to look at Thom Hark, and the expression on the Englishman's face showed he had heard it, as well. Culhane raised a finger to his lips. Hark nodded. In Culhane's right fist was the Detonics Scoremaster .45, cocked and locked. Culhane had figured that if the Vegas Crown invaders did have plastic explosives, the most economical system for total destruction of the hotel would be to topple the building. That required placing properly stemmed charges of explosives at strategic points against the vertical-support columns for the building, and all on one side. To produce the most damage, to tie up authorities longer, they would drop the structure into the street. The front of the building would be a logical site, but glass fronted the building for four stories and there would be no place to hide the charges. The last thing a saboteur wanted was to have his charges found easily.

The back of the complex would drop the hotel away from any streets. That meant one of the two sides. He judged the charges would have to be placed on either the second, third or fourth floor. Second or third would be best—the greater the mass of the building above the explosion, the more spectacular the results.

Knowledge was the ultimate fringe benefit from making one's living as a writer, he thought, albeit a peculiar body of knowledge at times. He possessed a modest reading command of Egyptian hieroglyphics, had once operated a hot-air balloon. He had spent almost an hour in a shark cage in the North Atlantic, had learned to remove venom from a diamondback rattler, could hot-wire most automobiles, had learned knife fighting from a true artist at the craft and—at least theoretically—knew how to knit. A female assassin in one of his novels had taken out her victims using curare-tipped knitting needles.

He stopped on the fourth-floor landing. From the third-floor landing below, he heard the clear voices, speaking in Russian.

Hark looked at him, his eyes asking what was being said. Culhane spoke Russian well enough, could read it barely at all, but could usually understand it quite well. He could understand these two men. But there was no way of translating for Thom Hark without betraying their position.

One of the men, with the deeper of the two voices, was complaining about Mordecai Nitsch. Nitsch had been wounded in his left leg by an older man. Culhane wondered if it had been Ed Morrison. He hoped that it had. But with Nitsch wounded, the man continued, and the robbery going so wrong from the start, could Nitsch get them out of here.

The other man, with a higher, slightly graveled voice, remarked that he had no intention of sitting around in the hotel while Nitsch blew it up. He'd go down fighting, take some hostages of his own and make a break for it. It was a big desert.

The conversation progressed with more details about Nitsch, how he seemed to be hot for someone named

Charlene, how they'd thought Nitsch and someone named Moishe Sebin would have had it out by now.

Culhane slowly holstered the Scoremaster. He removed the Bali-Song, one of the handmade ones with a Wee-Hawk blade, from the belt sheath. The middle finger of his right hand popped the locking block so the two handle halves would separate.

Culhane clamped the knife in his right fist, still unopened, and moved as soundlessly as he could to the edge of the landing, peering over the railing. The two Russian-speaking men were directly below him. He suddenly realized what he was dealing with—a group that was little known outside upper-echelon law-enforcement circles, the group referred to in the newspaper account he had read aboard the jetliner on his way to Vegas—he'd even saved the article for future reference as a book idea. The name had been given in the article. They were the Malina.

Culhane stepped over the landing railing, first the right leg, then the left. He extended his right leg to the staircase leading downward, following it with his left. With the Bali-Song in his teeth, he gripped the staircase railing with both hands.

The men were ten feet below him and to his left. Both had Uzi submachine guns, but neither man held his gun, and both weapons were casually slung.

Culhane turned around so his back would be to the railing.

He freed his right hand, removed the Bali-Song from his mouth and curled it in his right fist now.

Culhane jumped.

It wasn't the sort of thing to do in cowboy boots, but he landed without breaking an ankle, his body weight slamming into the gravelly voiced Russian. The Russian's knees buckled as he fell.

Culhane backstepped, catching his balance, as the second Russian brought his Uzi on line.

Culhane pivoted right on the ball of his right foot; his

left foot snapped out, slapping at the side of the second Russian's head in a double tae kwon-do kick. Pivoting one-hundred-eighty degrees, he found the terrorist's abdomen with his right foot and hammered the man back. The first Russian was up, and Culhane pitched himself toward the armed man, flicking open the Bali-Song as the Russian's Uzi came on line. The blade hacked down in a diagonal cut, slicing through the man's Adam's apple, and the tip of the blade ripped the carotid artery on the right side of the neck. The terrorist stared out in surprise and started to sink to his knees, his hands grasping for his throat. The man would be unconscious in under six seconds and dead in less than fifteen.

As the second Russian rose into a crouch, Culhane snapped out his right leg, and the sole of his boot slammed into the man's face.

Stepping forward, Culhane planted his left boot heavily on the Russian's inside right forearm, while his right hand brought his knife forward toward the terrorist's throat.

The Russian seemed halfway between consciousness and unconsciousness.

Culhane's right knee went against the man's chest as he leaned against him beside the stairwell wall. His right hand moved, and the Bali-Song rolled in his palm and he closed the knife.

The back of his left hand crashed down across the Russian's mouth. The Russian's eyes opened, the lids fluttering.

"Where are the explosives?" Culhane demanded. "Tell me—or so help me I'll tie you up and leave you in a closet somewhere, and when the explosives go, you go, too."

The Russian didn't hesitate. He jerked his head to the right, toward the door leading out of the stairwell. "There—bombs there. This side of hotel—only this floor. There."

"Are you part of the demolitions team? Answer me," and Culhane flicked open the Bali-Song again; it could be a good persuader.

"Yes—I fix bombs—not all, but I fix."

Culhane gestured with the knife again. "Now you unfix bombs—okay?"

The Russian didn't answer for a moment. Culhane suddenly realized that Thom Hark was beside him. He glanced at Hark for an instant before turning back to the Russian. "Either disarm those bombs—very carefully—or you'll die when they blow. Word of honor, pal—and you know Americans always keep their word."

"Yes—I will disarm."

With his left hand, Culhane began a quick frisk of his captive, discovering a Swiss-army knife, a Walther PP and a half-eaten Milky Way. He started to give back the candy bar, but thought better of it. It could have contained cyanide—at least it could have in one of his books.

THERE HAD BEEN NO GUARDS outside the service entrance to the hotel basement, but the door had been locked. The lock could have been shot away, but instead George picked it. While Track had been hospitalized after the final confrontation with Johannes Krieger, Chesterton had arranged a crash course in safe cracking and lock picking for George from an accomplished but retired British cat burglar. Evidently, Track thought, George had been a quick study. It took less than ninety seconds to have the dead-bolt lock opened.

"Since you opened it, I think it's only right you go in first," Track smiled and said as he stepped back from the doorway. "Anyway, you're bigger than I am and bullets won't hurt you as much."

"Bullshit! You just don't want to go through that door first—tell the truth. All right, I'll go. Send your poor nephew into the jaws of death, sure."

Track groaned. "Get away from the door," he said, and he put his hand to the steel knob and slowly twisted it.

There would be men inside—there had to be.

Track reached into the musette bag and pulled out the two sound-and-light grenades. "Hold this," he said to Wilson, passing him one of the SLGs.

Wilson looked at the grenade. "Sound-and-light grenades, right—Eggs?"

"Eggs," Track said as he nodded.

He had the pin out on one. "Pull the pin on the other one. George, you take the door. When I hit three, jerk it open, then hit the dirt and cover your ears."

"I'm the one who's used them, remember? Couldn't hear right for three days afterward."

George put his right hand on the door.

"Ready, Lew?" Track inquired. When Wilson nodded, Track continued his directive. "Ten seconds from impact and we go in fast and get them silently. Let the people on the first floor wonder what's going on. No sense making a lot of noise after the noise of these things. A gunshot sounds like a gunshot."

"Floors could be thick enough they might not even hear it. There's probably a lot of soundproofing on the casino floor, anyway," Wilson said.

Track nodded in agreement, then began the count. "One—two—three!"

George jerked the door open, and Track and Wilson hurled the Eggs through the opening. Then Track threw himself to the concrete, covering his ears with his hands, his eyes closed and his face turned from the building. The roar was still loud as the high-frequency sound blast echoed from the basement entrance.

"Six, one thousand seven, one thousand eight," Track counted to himself. "One thousand nine, one thousand ten!" He pushed himself up, the SPAS-12 on its sling at his right side and the silenced Walther P-5 pulled from the wide belt of his Levi's. As he kicked the door fully open, his left hand closed over the silencer tube, giving it a good-luck twist.

Inside, men rolled on the floor, staggered. One man, alert to the danger, was picking up a subgun.

Track pulled the trigger on the P-5 twice, and the man's body rocked with the twin 9mm hits to the mid-section; the subgun fell from his hands. George was decking a man to Track's left, and Wilson was using the butt of his Walther like a blackjack.

Track stepped toward another of the temporarily blinded and deafened Malina terrorists, aiming a fast knee raise to the man's crotch, then bringing the butt of the Walther across the back of the neck as the man doubled over.

Track wheeled around and counted six men on the floor. Two appeared to be dead; the others were moving slightly.

"George—check the bodies. Help them if you can, but search them first. Lew and I will head for the elevator shafts."

Track saw George nod and then started ahead toward the elevator shafts with Wilson beside him.

As they penetrated farther into the basement, Track realized that if there were any more Malina around, they would have been out of the effective range of the grenades and at least would be able to see.

"Your left—look out!" Wilson shouted.

Track wheeled left, to see a man coming out of the shadows by a stack of packing crates, holding an Uzi subgun. Track pumped the P-5's trigger twice, sending two silenced shots into the man's neck. The terrorist's head snapped back, his knees buckling, and the body sagged to the gray concrete floor.

"Thanks," Track said as he turned to Wilson.

Ahead was a stairwell, and an earlier look he'd had at

the architectural plans the police had provided told him it led to the subbasement and the elevator shafts.

"They know we're here if any of them are down there," Wilson commented.

"Yeah," Track agreed. "You stay by the top of the stairwell—I'm going down." Track gave the silencer a good-luck twist against the axis of the bore. He swapped the solitary spare magazine, having no desire to go into the subbasement with a half-empty pistol.

He started down.

Behind him Lew Wilson cracked, "Remember, be reckless!"

"Sure thing," Track rasped. He glanced at his watch. Less than a half-hour remained before the terrorists were to be paid their ransom—or detonate the bombs. But he had to neutralize Capezi's firebombs first.

He kept moving down the stairs.

There was no sound other than the pulse of the air-conditioning units from the mechanical room, which, from the intensity of the sound, appeared to be at the far end of the subbasement from the stairs.

Hugging the side of the wall, the Walther ready, he strained to listen—but the noises of the mechanical room were all he could hear. There was no time left for caution. He started ahead. Packing crates and miscellaneous machinery were stowed to his left; to his right stood dead or wounded roulette wheels, slot machines and other gambling paraphernalia.

He held the silenced P-5 close against his body to guard against a strike that would knock the pistol from his grasp. He felt the weight of the SPAS-12 on its sling against his side.

Dan Track kept walking.

The sound on his left of the packing crates moving alerted him, and he wheeled toward the sound, the Walther stabbing out for a target. Two men were coming for him, Uzis slung at their sides, knives in their hands. Track pumped the trigger of the Walther twice, and the nearer of the two men went down. As Track swung the extended muzzle toward the second man, something hammered at him from behind, and his knees buckled.

Track rolled forward as something crushed down on top of him.

The Walther slid from his right fist across the floor.

A combat boot was coming toward his face.

His left hand pinned under him, Track raised his right hand, grabbing at the boot as it came toward his face, deflecting the kick. But the foot aimed toward him again. His right hand protected his face, the wrist aching from the force of the kick. He bit down on the butt end of one of the *shuriken* spikes in the back of the glove, extracting it with his teeth. In one smooth motion, he took the spike in his hand and flicked it upward at the chest of his attacker. The boot hesitated in mid-kick, less than a foot from his face. Then the body stumbled back.

As Track freed his left hand, someone started hammering at his ribs with something hard.

He reached behind his back with his left hand, grabbing a handful of hair, twisting his fingers into it, tearing forward. He heard a shout of pain from his attacker.

The pressure on Track's back eased, and he turned, his right hand cupping his assailant's ear. He jerked at the ear and felt it ripping. The Malina terrorist screamed and tried to push the butt of his pistol into Track's neck.

Track threw his weight back and heard another scream. As he rolled onto his back, he could see half a human ear in his right hand.

The terrorist, blood gushing from the right side of his head, staggered back, reaching to his belt for a semi-automatic pistol.

Track's left hand moved to the Gerber MkII on his

left leg, catching at the orthopedically designed handle. He thrust the knife forward, underhanding it into the man's abdomen.

The man stood, swaying like a tree about to fall; then collapsed to the concrete floor, his pistol clattering down a split second before he himself hit the ground.

Track was up, gathering in his Walther. He walked over to one of the fallen terrorists and retrieved his *shuriken* throwing spike, wiping it clean on the man's chest before repositioning it in the sheath on the back of his glove.

Quickly he searched the three men, turning out their weapons and breaking down their guns. Only an idiot left guns behind him that could be turned against him. Track took back the Gerber, wiping it clean as well.

He picked up the two Uzis he'd taken from the knife wielders and continued across the subbasement. A quick look at his watch told him he'd have to speed things up—in twenty minutes Nitsch would detonate the C-4.

He took the corridor to his left, stopping, finding in the gray light the light switch, knowing he was at risk—the detonator could be wired to it. He hit the switch. Nothing happened except for the lights coming on.

He turned to face the base of the elevator bank. Grates covered the maintenance entrances to the shafts.

Track wheeled half left, and kicked against the lock with his right foot. The lock sprung, and he wrenched the grate open.

There was the faint smell of gasoline coming from the base of the shaft. "Oh, boy," he groaned.

26

As insurance that the captured Malina terrorist had completely disarmed the charges set against the four support columns in four separate rooms on the third floor, Culhane bound and gagged the man, securing him beside the last of the four charges. "Remember," he admonished, "if it goes, you go."

The man nodded.

Culhane turned to Hark, Dolore and Meadowshed beside the doorway. "That's it," he said. "And we've got about ten minutes before the ransom is to be paid."

"If we could make it down the stairwells into the basement, perhaps we could get outside and take up firing positions from there, right beside the building. We have enough guns for everyone now," Hark said.

Culhane nodded—it made sense. "Bob," he called out. "Ralph."

Both men turned from the doorway. "You guys have any objections to baby-sitting the third floor from here? If somebody comes up and rewires the charges, we're shit out of luck."

"I'll buy that," Meadowshed agreed.

Dolore only nodded.

Track turned to Thom Hark. "Since it was your idea, it only seems fair—"

"Yes." Hark nodded grimly. "I was afraid you were going to say that."

Culhane picked up the extra Uzi. Dolore and Meadowshed had two subguns apiece now, Hark one. "Let's go," Culhane told him. He turned to the bound-and-gagged Malina terrorist. "You have a nice evening, huh?"

Then with Hark beside him, Culhane started for the doorway.

MORDECAI NITSCH LOOKED AT HIS WRISTWATCH. Nine minutes remained before his ultimatum had to be met, and he was terrified. Killing all the people in the hotel did not disturb him. It was the thought of his own death.

He looked at the man who had shot him, stretched out on the crap table, and winced as pain raged through his own leg like a brushfire. The doctor in the rumpled gray suit had stopped the intestinal bleeding and was keeping the man alive. Nitsch understood the man had a chance of surviving. Once the man had babbled something about cancer in his pain.

Nitsch intended before leaving the hotel—either with his money aboard the buses that had rounded the corner and pulled up outside, or with a bullet to his own brain after the detonator activated—to shoot the man in the head and be done with him.

He felt that the KGB had betrayed him. Surely they had known that the sound of gunfire would activate special electronic alarms he had not realized existed in the Vegas Crown and that police would begin arriving almost instantly. He looked in the left breast pocket of his suit and took out the documents that would implicate the Israeli government. They would be found on his body, he reflected, not on the surreptitiously murdered body of Moishe Sebin, his rival with Charlene.

He sighed hard.

Eight minutes remained now. That was all to determine life or death for him.

IT WAS UNFAIR, Joe Capezi thought. But perhaps when the firebombs detonated, the men on the roof would panic, and he could run to his helicopter and still fly away.

He looked at his wristwatch—twenty-three minutes remained.

The demolitions expert had told him the effect of the bombs in the base of the elevator shafts would be similar to the old Jerry Lewis gag with the cigarette lighter, where the flame leaped so high it seemed impossible. The bombs would precipitate the same effect, with the elevator shafts serving as the lighter, the hotel itself sheathed in flame and the upper floors wicking the flame skyward. The fire would be impossible to extinguish. The hotel would be a total loss, and the heat of the flames would be so intense that all evidence of the incendiary bombs themselves would be obliterated. Even the detonators were encased in plastic so they would melt.

As he crouched beside the small, brightly painted cabana that was used to house the equipment for cleaning and testing the pool, he watched the dozen submachine-gun-armed men on the four sides of the roof and mentally ticked off what it would be necessary to do. Fly away. Not let the police find him. He would find *them*. His face filled with fear, bewilderment, shock and terror at the horror of the explosions.

But before encountering the police, he would have to find Jess Adolphi and the pilot, Tal Kelly. Likely Jess would have eliminated the pilot. But Jess needed to die very badly. And he would be a hard man to kill.

Capezi resolved to hold on to the submachine gun—it would give him the competitive edge over Adolphi and his pistol.

He waited—there was nothing else to do.

When the explosions came, he would run for the helicopter. There was no choice but to do that.

It was that or die the way everyone else in the hotel would die.

And the computer data banks that damned him to his father and to the Five Families would die, as well.

27

"Lew—you and George are going to have to go after the bombs the terrorists planted. We've got some time to play with—once they get the money, they have to check it with that equipment they asked for and then they have to get themselves on to the buses. They won't let the hotel go up until they're on the way to the airport and the hotel's filled with cops and hostages—the more they can kill, the better."

Track had disarmed seven of the devices so far—nine remained. Eight and one-half, really, he thought. He had removed the visible detonator from the ten-or-so pounds of the C-4 and was probing into the plastique itself with the long blade of his Gerber MkII. "When you search for the terrorist bombs, be on the lookout for hidden detonators like these."

"They hide them so that when you find the exposed detonator—" George began.

"Exactly," Track said over his shoulder to George. Then he looked back to the plastique. "You take all the trouble to mine something like a bridge with explosives, then say a sentry sees you and you make a run for it. He sees one detonator exposed, disconnects it. Then he goes on and finds the rest of the charges and disconnects those detonators. That gives you time to get away while the detonators tick on—the ones that were hidden inside the explosives. Then you just find a nice safe spot and watch them blow. Whoever did this, did about everything you can do to make one of these things work except install trembler switches—you guys have got to watch closely for those when you find the explosives the Malina have planted.''

"What the hell are 'trembler switches'?" he heard Wilson ask. Wilson and George were removing the ammonium nitrate, painter's-grade aluminum powder and the plastic jerricans of gasoline from the as-yet-functional bombs in the eight remaining elevator shafts. To hear one another over the hum of the motors that ran the ventilation system, it was necessary to shout.

"Trembler switches would have made this a no-option situation. These things are called FAE bombs—acronym for Fuel Air Explosion. The C-4 explodes, and the ammonium nitrate and the aluminum powder burn hot enough to stay burning so the force of the explosion doesn't blow out the fire. They ignite the gasoline and go up like a torch, with the flames rising, seeking oxygen. The entire building would be gone. With trembler switches, you touch the detonator, you activate the trembler switch, and sixty seconds later—no matter what you do—the detonator activates and you have your explosion.''

Track found the hidden detonator in the plastique, and warmed the plastique in his hands to make it more malleable in order to free the detonator enough to snip the wires.

"What if we find trembler switches? How will we know them?" George asked.

"If you find them before you realize what they are and touch them, you'll know them when the bomb goes up in your face. They're usually yellow plastic these days. Should look like an add-on at the side of the detonator. But it won't always—sometimes they're built into the detonator.''

"Then—" Wilson began.

"I could have blown us all up—you got it. One of these could still have a trembler on it," Track announced, freeing the hidden detonator and snipping the wires with the edge of the Gerber. Track exhaled, standing up and flexing his cramped shoulder muscles. "If you detect a trembler switch, leave it alone. And in the comforting thoughts department," Track added, turning, walking away from the elevator bank and starting to the second bank and the eight remaining detonation systems, "our little friend Capezi could have put a trembler into one of these."

Track rolled back the cuff of his bomber jacket. "I make it we've got twenty-one minutes before these detonators activate," he said, looking at his watch. "And since you guys are needed elsewhere, let's chat later, okay? I've got less than three minutes per bomb, and that doesn't leave me a lot of spare time."

Track turned toward the nearest elevator shaft and set to work, glancing back over his shoulder once as Wilson and George left for the staircase leading up to the basement.

He removed the visible detonator, clipping the wires. It was functional, but set for two minutes later than the actual concealed detonators in each of the charges had been set for. They were "set-as-you-will" timers built from parts—well built—and using quartz-crystal oscillator chips. They were as efficient as photo timers, less traceable and cheaper. Track set the exposed timer down beside him and began probing with the Gerber to find the hidden timer.

There was always the possibility that the hidden timers he had located were there for him to locate and there was some other detonation system hidden deeper in the ten-or-so pounds of plastique that made up the basic explosive charge. If that was the case, he wouldn't have the time to exit the subbasement before detonation, because it was likely this third timing system would be advanced over the timers he was finding buried in the plastique.

Track shrugged. Demolitions work could be routine,

or "as hazardous as walking a greased tightrope, blind-folded, fifty feet in the air," his old friend the demolitions expert had once remarked. This was somewhere in between.

Dan Track located the hidden timer and was kneading the plastique when he heard a sound on the staircase behind him.

He wheeled, still crouched, the little Trapper Scorpion .45 coming into his fist, already cocked and locked, the safety whipping down as he thrust the dull, nickel-finished pistol toward the stairs.

Track halted the trigger squeeze. It was George. There was a grin on his nephew's face. "You know that Takers book you made me read, the one written by Josh Culhane?"

"Yeah." Track nodded, not understanding.

"Well—you'll never guess who Lew and I bumped into," and George motioned to the stairs.

Track had seen his face dozens of times, listened to the man, watched him in television interviews. He was tall, lean but well muscled. The overhead light at the base of the stairs brought out some red in his brown hair. In his right fist gleamed a Detonics Scoremaster .45, just like the one Sean Dodge used in the books.

George was talking again. "And you'll never guess what your author friend was up to. He and this other guy—"

"Thom Hark, actually," a bespectacled, sandy-brown-haired man standing beside Culhane announced. The accent was decidedly English, the tone of voice slightly amused.

"They disarmed the devices planted on the third floor—the Malina bombs. We're home free!"

Track stood up, thumbing up the safety on the Trapper .45 and holstering it in the little Alessi inside holster beside his right kidney. He started to laugh. "You know, I've always wanted to meet you, Culhane—I'm one of your biggest fans. But right now, we've still got seven biggees to go down here.'' Track looked at Wilson. ''Lew—give me a hand on these.'' He looked at Culhane. ''How good are you with explosives?'' he asked.

Culhane's voice was low, even. ''You tell me what needs doing and how you're doing it—you've got an extra set of hands.''

Track looked at George. ''George—you and Mr. Hark get by the stairwells leading up to the casino and keep them covered. We'll knock these off.'' Track looked at Wilson. ''Lew—show Mr. Culhane what we've been doing,'' and he turned to Culhane. ''Concealed detonators—like you used in Takers number eight.''

''It was number seven.'' Culhane grinned. ''But I get the picture.''

Track turned to the next device—seven remained. Wilson should be able to get two of them, Track thought. And if Culhane was half as good as Sean Dodge, he could get another two. That left Dan Track with three.

As he worked, cutting away the exposed detonator, then kneading the plastique to make it easier for the Gerber to probe, he talked. ''We met Mary Frances Mulrooney.''

''Fanny? Where?'' he heard Culhane asking.

''Fanny—cute name. She's outside. Safe enough. Nailed some guy named Adolphi out in the desert. And some guy named—'' He looked behind him to the opposite side of the elevator bank to Lew Wilson. ''What the hell was that pilot's name, Lew?''

''I don't know if she told us, but if she did, I must've forgotten.''

Track nodded, looking back to his explosive. He was already probing with the Gerber. ''Anyway, there was some story about a pilot. She killed Adolphi—gutsy girl.''

"She's all right?"

"Yeah, she's fine, Mr. Culhane."

"Josh will do. Who the hell are you—feds?"

"I'm Dan Track and he's Lew Wilson. I'm with an outfit called the Consortium—a cartel of international insurance underwriters. They insure this place."

"Sort of the Johnny Dollar of the 1980s, huh?"

Track laughed at the comparison to the radio detective. "You've got a good memory—yeah. Lew's a special agent with the Florida Department of Law Enforcement. He's had considerable experience with the Malina."

"Then that's who these assholes are," he heard Culhane saying.

"Yeah, you should send Sean Dodge up against them some time," Track said.

"Maybe I will. Maybe you guys can help him."

Track snipped the detonator wires and moved in a crouch to the next charge. "That'd be okay, wouldn't it, Lew—see ourselves in an adventure novel?"

He heard Wilson laugh. "Yeah, that'll be the day."

Track snipped the wires of the exposed detonator and started to work the plastique. "Anyway, Miss Mulrooney learned that Joe Capezi—the son of Crazy Carlo Capezi the Mafia Don—"

"Capezi owns this place, right—some kind of front for the Five Families?" Culhane interrupted.

"Not much of a front," Wilson interjected. "Everybody knows about it—there, got the sucker. They had that detonator buried deep."

"Anyway," Track continued, "Capezi had been embezzling a lot of money. He had his accounting in his computer and the mob was hacking the computer—"

"Hackers in the mob?" Culhane asked.

"Yeah, stealing the data. That's why he planned to torch the hotel. Burn up his computer—there's no data left to rob. The sudden appearance of the Malina gave him perfect cover."

"These things couldn't have been set before the Malina attacked," Culhane was saying.

"You know, Dan, he's got a point," Wilson said. "Means our boy Capezi is loose in the hotel somewhere."

Track nodded grimly, snipping the wires of the concealed detonator. "How you guys coming along?"

"I'm working on my second one," Wilson volunteered.

"Just snipping the wires on my first and moving on," Culhane acknowledged. "How we doing on time?"

"Not too hot," Track told them without looking at his watch. "But not too bad, either. I make it about ten minutes, maybe eight. We'll get them unless one of these is wired different. And I don't think so."

"I saw all that gasoline and the painter's aluminum powder—these were going to be FAE bombs?"

"You really do do your homework." Track laughed. "Yeah, FAE bombs. Make the whole hotel a torch. But we moved the gasoline out. All we've got to do is keep the plastique from blowing us up. What kind of stuff were they using upstairs?"

"Had C-4 stemmed with bags of ready-mix concrete shaped to the support posts for the hotel on one side."

"Hey, I was right." Track nodded, glancing over his shoulder to Wilson.

"A tip of the hat to Major Track," Wilson cracked.

"Major? Army?" Culhane inquired.

"CID for almost fifteen years," Track told Culhane. "Just Mr. Track these days."

"You guys have any plans for the Malina?" Culhane asked. "When we worked our way down the stairwell, we could see them getting their money delivered. The bombs were wired to go by radio detonation, so they probably don't know Thom and Bob Meadowshed and Ralph Dolore and I knocked them out yet. And Meadowshed and Dolore are upstairs guarding the third floor to keep them from fixing the stuff so they can detonate the plastique again—you know, rewiring it.''

Track snipped his last two wires. "Done," he announced. He stood up, his muscles cramped. "Either of you guys need any help?"

Wilson stood up, too. "No, I just got mine. That's it.''

Culhane, still working, his back turned to Track, murmured, "Almost got it—easier when I write about this stuff.''

Track nodded superfluously. "You wanted to know if I had some plans for the Malina. Well, let me ask you something. How would you like to help?"

Culhane looked up, stood, flicking closed what Track recognized as a Bali-Song knife. "Yeah, I'd love to help.''

"Okay," Track said, "quick quiz. Tell me all you know about C-4."

Culhane nodded. "Safe to light a cigarette?"

"Yeah, just don't go extinguishing it in the gasoline cans. I know some guys like to be show-offs.''

Culhane shrugged. "Okay, C-4 stands for Cyclotrimethylenetrinitramine—sometimes called Cylconite. It's composed of RDX and modifiers and was developed in Great Britain some years ago. Let's see, you can't chew it because it's poisonous—"

"Think." Track grinned.

"And you can't inhale it if it's burning," Culhane said suddenly. "Because the fumes—"

"The fumes will get you high as a kite." Track concluded for him. "When it was first used in Vietnam, they used to tell the guys it was safe to cook over—"

Wilson interrupted Track, "But then they had to retract the manual because the guys would inadvertently inhale the fumes in a tent or something—"

"And they'd be drunk," Culhane finished.

Track nodded. "How about we get some of the C-4,

bring it over by the air-conditioning units in the mechanical room, open up some panels and burn some of it, then fan it into the air-conditioning ducts,'' Track said. "Lew, you shout up for George to throw down his gas mask and stay by an open door with Thom Hark." He turned to Culhane. "This is going to put your friends Meadowshed and Dolore out of whack for a while, too, but it can't be helped."

Culhane shrugged. "For a good cause—they won't mind when they find out. Let's do it," he said.

"I knew there was a reason I liked your books."

28

Moishe Sebin took the restarted elevator along with six men to the third floor. Mordecai Nitsch had checked the radio signal to the detonators and was getting an indication of a malfunction.

Nitsch suspected the four men who had escaped in the elevator before the elevators had been shut down. They had never been found, and one of his men, Strakwitz, had been missing ever since.

Sebin, his six men around him, exited the elevator into the corridor. Because one of the men, like himself, was a native Israeli and spoke no Russian and the other five spoke little or no Hebrew, Sebin told them in English, "These men are armed, remember, and evidently know how to use weapons. According to the others we interrogated, they are adventure novelists. But do not let such an occupation lull you into thinking they may not be dangerous."

He left the small corridor that led to the elevator banks and entered the main hallway.

There was a sudden burst of submachine gunfire—it was from an Uzi, a sound he had been familiar with nearly all his adult life.

He felt the sound, as well as heard it, feeling the heat and then almost instantly the cold in the pit of his stomach. His body slapped back against the corridor wall as he tried swinging his own Uzi forward.

But his arms weren't working.

There was gunfire all around him now. His own men were firing back. Ari, the other Israeli, was down, his

Uzi discharging uselessly into the carpeted floor. One of the Russians was down, his Uzi slung at his side, his pistol firing once as he fell.

Sebin slipped all the way to the floor, toppling over, raising his head. He had seen the fleeting image of a dark-haired young man at one side of the corridor. At the other end was a blond-haired man with a mustache. They had him and his men in a cross fire. Sebin's body rocked with another burst of subgun fire, but he still could not move his arms to get to a weapon. Another of the Russians was down.

They were all going down. The rattle of subgun fire was deafening in the corridor. Chunks of the wall pelted down on him.

He closed his eyes.

He started to whisper Charlene's name, but nothing worked anymore. He opened his eyes, and for an instant the image of death all around him was frozen in his consciousness. . . .

29

George Beegh and Thom Hark waited, inhaling in turns as they would face the open door leading from the basement, then turning back to guard the stairwell. The fumes from the C-4 were thick in the air, and George could not associate the smell with anything he had ever smelled before.

His uncle, Lew Wilson and Josh Culhane had been burning the C-4 in the subbasement and feeding it into the ventilation system for fifteen minutes now.

Hark turned away to breathe, coughed and asked, "How much longer, George?"

"Maybe another couple of minutes. Then we run up the stairwell and start shooting," George answered, turning to gulp fresh air.

"If they are all immobilized, then won't that be like committing murder in cold blood?"

George looked away from the stairwell, gulping air again. "A couple of dozen homicidal drunks all armed with submachine guns, completely disoriented and probably realizing all this is happening intentionally can't exactly be considered innocent and defenseless." He turned back to face the stairwell.

George heard Hark say, "I suppose you're right, but it won't affect us?"

"Dan's going to set the system to maximum and it'll blow out the rest of the fumes while we're heading up the stairwell. We might get headaches for our trouble, but that'll be about it. No cheap drunk, I'm afraid."

He turned back to the stairwell as Hark turned away.

He heard the Englishman say, "Pity, I'd been looking forward to that part of it."

George could see his uncle running up the stairs, gas mask in place. Wilson and Culhane were just behind him.

Track waved toward George.

George turned away from the stairwell, taking a radio set from his belt, hearing static in his earphone as he moved the wire. He'd have it looked at later for a short. "This is George, Sir Abner, come in."

"Chesterton here, go ahead, dear boy."

"We're going in, be ready. George out."

"Good luck! Chesterton out."

George replaced the radio in the belt holster, keeping the earphone in place. He took one long deep breath to get him up the stairwell, then broke into a dead run, following his uncle, Wilson, Culhane and Hark. George's M-16 was gripped tightly in both fists at high port.

HE'D WATCHED IT as it had happened. Men had suddenly burst into fits of laughter, then pushed and shoved at one another. Charlene had run to him, giddy fits of laughter bubbling from her lips. He knew what it was. They were burning the C-4 and had somehow got it into the ventilation system.

He ordered some of the men beside him to stop counting and examining the money and accompany him to the elevators. Two of them were to drag Charlene.

Limping on his good right leg, the wound in his left leg open from the exertion and bleeding again, he realized it was the adrenaline built up in his system from the pain that was keeping him sober enough at least to think.

"The elevator isn't coming, Mordecai—that's a cute name." Charlene laughed. "Elevator is a cute name, too. English is such a funny language. We will elevate ourselves—very, very soon." She giggled.

He was feeling the light-headedness. It made him reckless—he had forgotten to take any of the money with him.

"Charlene, you can't talk like that," he said. His tongue was thick, and he slurred his words. He shook his head, trying to clear the fog that was enveloping his mind. He hammered his left fist against the wound in the top of his left thigh. The pain almost made him faint, but it cleared his head for an instant. He pushed the elevator button and watched helplessly as the six men who had come with him to the elevator banks started to fight among themselves. There was sporadic submachine gunfire coming from the casino.

They were drunken animals, he realized, useless to him.

But there was a helicopter on top of the roof, and if he could sober Charlene enough, she could fly it.

He punched at his wound again to keep himself going. There was no elevator yet.

"It will come, Mordecai—I have faith. Did you know, Mordecai, that it is a very good thing to have faith? Faith can move mountains. Can faith move an elevator, Mordecai?"

He looked at her, his head reeling the way it would from cheap wine drunk too fast in the desert heat. He slapped her face to startle her. She laughed.

He laughed, too. Still there was no elevator.

30

Track hit the top of the stairwell, ripping away the gas mask, half choking on the smell of the air, but the air conditioning would blow it out before there was enough time for him to breathe a sufficient quantity to affect him.

Lew Wilson was beside him. As he looked back he saw Culhane, George and the Englishman Hark.

Track swung the SPAS-12 forward, running from the stairwell door down the long corridor that led past the elevator banks and to the casino. Ahead of him was gunfire, screaming and laughter—insane howls of laughter.

A half dozen of the Malina were blocking the corridor, none of them paying attention to him, he realized, all of them arguing among themselves. Track leveled the SPAS-12, set on semiautomatic, loaded with a full magazine of double O buck.

It wasn't murder, he told himself. They were lunatics, armed with submachine guns and to a man accountable for misery and grief from Russia and Israel to New York, Los Angeles, Miami and points in between.

His trigger finger edged the combat safety forward from the guard, then snapped back against the trigger itself. One man went down, then another and another. The men were turning to face him as he ran headlong toward them, their subguns rising, one of the men already firing. Track worked the trigger of the SPAS and a load of buck tore into the face and neck of the subgunner, almost decapitating him.

shuriken spikes to down a charging, drunken, wildly shooting Malina. But Culhane was wheeling around, the Scoremaster flashing outward, firing a professional 2-shot semiauto tap. The subgunner spun away, pirouetting wildly, then crashed down.

Track edged closer to the others; Wilson and Hark were somewhere—he wasn't sure where.

George shouted. "As soon as we hit the corridor, I called Sir Abner on the radio. The cops and the military should be in here in a second!"

Track nodded, ramming a fresh magazine into his own .45. He holstered the Trapper, starting to feed more rounds into the SPAS.

George had the M-16 now and was firing.

"Give me the Walther—the subgun," Track snapped.

George shrugged out of the sling, passing the subgun to Track.

Track could see Wilson and Hark now, pinned down by the mezzanine bar. A half dozen of the Malina gunmen were having what looked like lunatic target practice, laughing, howling gleefully as they fired into the bar.

"Let's go," Track shouted. He was up, running, the Walther MPK in both fists spitting fire as he advanced on the mezzanine bar. He could see Hark and Wilson more clearly now, and he realized they saw him. They were up, counterattacking.

The Malina were caught in a cross fire as Track's subgun stuttered in his hands, while to his right George fired the M-16 and on his left Culhane stroked his .45, its repeated boom almost like a pulse.

The Malina were all concentrated in the bar area as Track, Culhane and George consolidated with Wilson and Hark.

Behind them, toward the front of the casino, gunfire echoed off the glass and shouted commands over bullhorns flooded the air.

Wilson quipped, "Looks like the Marines are landing."

"But not in time—look there!" Hark shouted.

Track wheeled. Behind him, on the far end of the elevator banks, he could see an elevator-shaft door closing.

"I'm going to get them, whoever the hell they are," Track shouted, starting to run. He threw George the nearly empty Walther MPK subgun. "They must be going for the chopper on the roof—one of them must be able to fly it!"

George fell in beside him as Wilson shouted, "Hey, don't go without me!"

Track looked back once. Culhane and Hark were running toward the front of the casino, where most of the hostages had been. He understood why. As they had fanned the fumes of the burning C-4 into the air-conditioning system, Culhane had told him. There was a man among the hostages who had likely wounded Mordecai Nitsch—a writer like Culhane, but a man Culhane looked on almost as a father.

Some things were more important than going after the bad guys—at least in real life, Track told himself.

They hit the elevator bank as one of the elevators was just closing.

Track threw himself against the door, blocking it, and Wilson and George poured inside. Track sagged away from the door, out of breath, and the doors snapped shut.

Wilson had the panel open under the floor buttons. "Hang on—I'm expressing it now!"

Track could already feel the motion in the pit of his stomach.

THE SMALLER DETONICS COMBAT MASTER, the action still locked open over the emptied magazine, was stuffed in the front of his Levi's. As he ran, Culhane rammed a fresh magazine up the butt of the Scoremaster. Hark was beside him. Sounding breathless, his editor snapped, "Looking for Morrison or the marketing man?"

"What the hell do you think?" Culhane answered.

A Malina terrorist appeared to Culhane's left and he made to shoot, but Hark shot faster, shoving Culhane back as he rammed the Uzi across Culhane's abdomen and fired a 3-round burst, then another and another.

The Malina subgunner went down in a bloodied heap.

Culhane ran ahead, reloading the little Detonics with one of the magazines for the Scoremaster. With both guns in his hands, he hit the far side of the casino, where Ed Morrison had been on the crap table.

"Ed! Ed!"

There was fighting on all sides of them—the insanely high Malina fighters not surrendering and the hostages shrieking wildly with alternating spasms of horror and laughter.

Culhane saw Morrison roll off the table, struggling on the floor as he tried to crawl, one hand holding his guts in. He started toward him. "Ed!"

Three of the Malina came at them. Hark fired, and one man went down. "Damn thing's out of ammo!" he screamed.

Culhane took up the slack, and his pistols barked, two shots apiece, boring deep into the midsections of the Malina gunmen.

To his right there was a blur of motion, no time to fire, something hammering at him. Culhane rolled with it, falling, both pistols loosening in his grip for an instant. He looked up to see one of the Malina hovering over him, while a second one grappled with Hark. Culhane rolled onto his back, his right hand finding the butt of the Scoremaster. He stabbed the weapon forward, firing it into the face of the subgunner.

The man seemed frozen in midstep. Then he suddenly toppled backward.

Hark was hammering his Uzi into the face of the second Malina subgunner, and the man sank to his knees, then fell on his side, his face a bloody mass of pulped flesh and bone.

Culhane was up, took three steps and was beside Morrison, shielding the man with his own body as best he could. "You'll be all right—it's okay—it's over now."

Morrison was just laughing, drunk on the gas from the C-4. With each spasm of laughter the stain of blood on the carpet seemed to grow, darker red against red.

31

The elevator doors opened, and Track thrust the SPAS through the doorway, into the corridor, trying to pin down any opposition. There was no answering fire.

George stepped out into the hallway, his Walther MPK swinging right to left, hunting a target. Lew Wilson, an M-16 held tightly in both fists, was beside him.

The elevators normally would not travel above the twenty-fourth floor, but when Wilson had pried away the cover over the operating controls, they were able to express the elevator all the way to twenty-eight.

It was conceivable, Track realized, reloading the SPAS, that whoever had taken the elevator up had not gone to the roof. Conceivable, but doubtful.

To his right he could see what looked to be a sealed section of the floor. The large wooden office doors were apparently once locked closed, but the locks were shot off and the doors were open wide.

"That way," Track murmured to Lew Wilson and George Beegh. "And remember, there were at least twelve guys up here to begin with. They'll know it's gone bad, and they didn't get exposed to the gas from the C-4."

The safety on the SPAS-12 was off, and Track had eight rounds in the magazine and one more in the chamber.

Track held the SPAS, its stock collapsed, close beside him as he moved toward the office doorway. George was to his right, the Walther MPK 9mm subgun in his right hand, the Smith & Wesson 469 in his left.

In Wilson's right hand was the M-16 assault rifle, in his left the Beretta 92SB, his issue gun with the Florida Department of Law Enforcement.

A gun in each hand wasn't a bad idea, Dan Track thought. He shifted the SPAS entirely to his right hand, tensioning it from his body against the sling for added support. Using his left hand, he awkwardly drew the freshly reloaded Metalife Custom L-Frame .357 revolver from the shoulder rig under his left armpit.

There was no sound ahead, except for the distant moan of emergency vehicle sirens filtering up from twenty-eight stories below.

Track slowly passed through the doorway.

"Where the hell are they?" Wilson asked.

"Out on the roof," Track whispered.

Dan Track moved ahead, the SPAS-12 ready in his right fist, the L-Frame Smith ready in his left.

There were glass doors leading to a veranda. The glass was shot out. A pool was visible beyond.

Across the roof, beyond the pool, stood a helicopter, the rotors idling lazily. Track could count as many as twenty figures standing around it, like worshippers standing dumbly at a disappointing shrine.

"It can't take off, I bet," George said.

Track glanced once to his nephew. He said nothing.

They were on borrowed time until one of the Malina turned around and spotted them. Track could clearly that one of the terrorists was having a difficult time standing. It would be the leader, he thought, Mordecai Nitsch. Nitsch reportedly had some sort of leg wound.

Track stepped over the broken glass in the doorframes, advancing. The dying sun was hot on his flesh as he walked toward the pool, his eyes flickering right to left to right, searching out cover. Aside from a utility box disguised as a cabana on the far side of the pool, there was none except the pool itself.

Track stopped, and Wilson and George flanked him.

He pushed the Metalife Custom .357 into his waistband, nodding to George and to Wilson.

Wilson shook his head. "The badge," he rasped, his voice barely audible.

Track nodded to him. Wilson was a lawman. Track realized he should remember that, too. He nodded again to Wilson, then gestured with his head toward the knot of helicopter worshippers.

Track heard Wilson clear his throat. "Police officers!" Wilson shouted the words. "Freeze—you're under arrest!"

Before the terrorists wheeled and the gunfire started, Wilson laughed and said, "I just deputized both you guys!"

George headed out laterally; Wilson moved to the opposite flank.

As the subgun fire started, Track triggered the SPAS-12, hitting the deck beside the pool. He went into a roll as bursts of subgun fire ripped chunks out of the masonry, the spray of concrete dust a cloud in the air as he worked the trigger of the SPAS as fast as he could. There was subgun fire to one side of him, where George stood with the MPK. The sharper crack of assault rifle fire came from Wilson's M-16. The Malina, caught by surprise, were going down. Those still standing dispersed to the area beyond the rooftop helipad.

"Let's go," Track shouted, pushing himself up, ramming more rounds into the tubular magazine of the SPAS. He jumped the corner of the pool as subgun fire rooster-tailed across the water's surface.

With the helicopter fifty yards away, Track saw a group of Malina to his right, cutting around the corner of the raised superstructure of the office and living quarters.

Track skidded on his heels, turning after them, shot from the SPAS sending up clouds of powdered concrete from the corner of the building. He looked behind him once to the helicopter. The bubble dome was shattered from subgun fire, and sprawling half out of the dome was a body, bullet wounds visible all over the face and the light-colored suit coat. The eyes were wide open in death.

He heard Wilson shout from behind him, "So much for Joe Capezi—the Malina must've zapped him when he made a break for it with the chopper."

Track looked back again. He remembered a phrase the late Ian Fleming had used: "Rough justice."

For Joe Capezi, the man who would have torched his own hotel, killing hundreds in order to cover his crimes from his father, "rough justice" was the most appropriate kind.

Track started after the escaping Malina. He reached the corner of the rooftop superstructure, flattening himself against it. Then he waved the muzzle of the SPAS around the corner, drawing it back quickly as subgun fire tore into the concrete. Wilson and George were beside him.

"Want me to cut around through the offices here— maybe get out behind them?" Wilson asked.

Track looked at his old friend. "Better still, take this," and Track handed Wilson the SPAS, unslinging it. "George, give him the MPK, too."

"What—I'm going to charge them alone?" Wilson asked.

Track shook his head, grinning. "You keep them busy from here. Lob a few rounds from the SPAS, a few rounds from the Walther, maybe a magazine full from your M-16. Give us about five minutes, then come around through the office—we should be engaging the enemy by then. Just remember to bring my SPAS with you, okay?"

Wilson laughed. "You're fond of this thing, aren't you?" and he gestured with the Franchi police shotgun.

"Yeah. Good luck," and Track slapped Wilson on

the back. "Come on, George." Track started running, back toward the pool, a pistol in each hand. George held the M-16 in his right fist and the Smith 469 Mini-Gun in his left.

From behind them, Track could hear the boom of the SPAS, then the rattle of George's MPK. They reached the shattered glass doors beyond the swimming pool, stepping through into the office. Track took the right side of the room, George the left side, advancing toward the doors leading to the corridor.

Track could see movement beyond the windows in the office on the far side of the floor. Keeping his voice low, he called to George, "They only have one shot, and it's suicide—the elevators down to the subbasement. Maybe they'll figure they can shoot their way out."

The movement near the office was more definite now, and the air cracked with the sounds of glass shattering as windows were broken. Track had been ticking off the seconds. Wilson had two more minutes of keeping them busy. It should work out just right.

George whispered, "Do we move?"

"Wait—in a minute or so they'll be in the corridor by the elevator banks." He could see well enough to count as the Malina entered through the shattered windows in the far office. There was a woman, and the man with the bad leg. It would be Mordecai Nitsch. Track counted five others. Track guessed they had left two or three behind to cover their backs. He was still mentally ticking the seconds. About another minute before Wilson broke off. The other two or three Malina would do the same.

Three of the Malina were into the corridor, sweeping it with their Uzis, but not firing. Track heard a guttural shout from near the far side office, and Mordecai Nitsch, the woman and the two others emerged from the office. One of the pointmen was pressing the elevator call button.

Thirty seconds remained before Wilson would come and the shooting would start.

Track snapped his fingers once to get George's attention.

One of the Malina turned around quickly, as if hearing something, then looked away.

George glanced toward Track. Track gestured toward the M-16, then pointed to the men near the elevator.

George nodded, stuffed the Smith into his belt and raised the M-16. Turning on the Aimpoint sight, he settled the rifle to his shoulder, and Track watched as George adjusted the dial of the potentiometer.

George looked at him once.

Track nodded. Wilson would be coming.

George fired a 3-round burst—one of the men beside the elevator banks went down—then another burst, bringing another man down.

Track shouted to him, "Don't see what the hell you need me around for, George—what a hot-rock marksman!" and Dan Track started to run into the corridor as George unleashed another 3-round burst, and another of the Malina went down.

Subgun fire came back now from the woman and the one man with her and Mordecai Nitsch.

Track fired the pistols in his fists, diving to the shelter of a steel office desk.

He rolled, his back to the desk, the sounds of slugs thudding into the metal beating out a deadly tattoo. He rammed a fresh magazine into the Trapper Scorpion and reloaded the L-Frame with a fresh Safariland speedloader.

He could see Wilson running through the patio doors from the pool. The SPAS thundered twice and was silent. There was a scream from beside the elevator banks.

Track pushed himself up, firing out the Scorpion .45 as he ran for the cover of the next desk.

Subgun fire ripped into the ceiling over his head and into the desks surrounding him.

He looked back. Wilson and George were coming, each firing their M-16s. Track peered around the pedestal of the desk. One of the elevator doors was opening, then a second.

The woman, her left sleeve stained red with blood, and the limping man, disappeared into the farthest elevator.

Track fired toward them. A slug from the L-Frame in his left fist nailed one of the Malina.

Wilson and George were up even with him, firing toward the elevator banks. The door to the elevator was slamming closed, then reopening, closing, opening.

"Give me the SPAS!" Track shouted to Wilson. The riot shotgun sailed toward him, and Track snatched it in midair with his right fist while Wilson and George traded shots with the Malina who had provided the covering fire for Nitsch, the woman and the other terrorists.

"Get them," Track snarled as he ran for the elevator bank. The doors of the two elevators were still opening and slapping closed.

Subgun fire poured from the farthest of the two elevators, and Track hurled his body into the nearer one as the doors slammed shut again. This time they didn't reopen. Spread-eagled on the elevator floor, Track could feel the motion. He was dropping downward. The wall to his right suddenly ripped through with submachine gunfire. Nitsch and the woman were shooting at him from the next car as they plummeted.

Track edged the SPAS forward, searching his left flap pocket, finding the Federal Super Slugs and ramming them into the magazine of the emptied SPAS.

He crawled across the floor, reaching up to the elevator controls. It was the same elevator Wilson had piloted to the top floor by breaking into the elevator control panel. Track reached up with his left hand, pushing the button marked S-BMT. It stood for the sub-basement, where Nitsch and the woman had to be heading.

More subgun fire ripped through the walls of the elevator, and chunks of metal, fabric and plastic sprayed everywhere around him.

There was no place to take cover.

Track edged into the farthest corner, firing the SPAS. The noise was deafening in the confined space of the elevator. The Super Slugs tore gaping holes in the elevator wall—into the next car, as well, he hoped. He fed more rounds into the SPAS, firing again as fresh bursts of subgun fire came through the wall at him. The 9mms ricocheted off corners of the elevator walls, whining, screeching in the confined space. Projectiles zipped past him like blood-hungry insects on a damp summer night, passing inches from his ears. He fired the SPAS, jerking the trigger as fast as his finger could move, making patterns in the elevator wall, zigzagging, then breaking the patterns so he could catch Nitsch and the woman.

The elevator came to a sudden, violent stop.

The doors sprang open.

Track rammed more shells into the magazine of the SPAS.

He was on his knees. There was no shooting; not a sound came from the outside corridor.

The elevator doors began to close, and Track pushed himself up and dived through. The doors popped open, then slapped shut, then popped open again. Through the opening into the companion car, he could see the woman, her body smeared with blood, sagging against the elevator wall.

Track looked to his right across the subbasement.

Movement—Nitsch.

"Freeze!" Track yelled. He'd been hanging around Wilson too long.

Mordecai Nitsch threw himself from behind some

dead slot machines, his left trouser leg drenched with blood. Wounds were visible across the top of his right shoulder and near the right side of his abdomen.

But in his left hand was a Mini-Uzi.

The Uzi started to chatter.

Dan Track rasped, "Goodbye," and pulled the trigger of the SPAS-12. Nitsch's body rocked with the impact. Track pulled the trigger again. The Uzi still fired as Nitsch fell back. Track pulled the trigger again, then again and again. The Uzi suddenly went silent. Nitsch's head seemed to explode as the body slapped against one of the slot machines and stood there.

Track advanced, feeding more rounds into the SPAS.

He pulled up less than two yards from Nitsch. The collar of the would-be-mass-murderer's blood-smeared khaki coat had caught on the handle of the machine.

As Track watched the body twitched—a muscle spasm. Nitsch was already dead. The body slipped downward and the handle of the slot machine pulled down.

But nothing happened; no small fortune in coins sprayed out to cover the dead man.

Track turned away, murmuring, "Only in books. He didn't even get three oranges."

EPILOGUE

Dan Track sat in a penthouse restaurant in another Las Vegas hotel. On his plate were two barely cooked sunny-side-up eggs, hash browns and a small steak. He took a sip of his orange juice. He'd spent an hour that morning talking with Don Carlo Capezi, and the thing that still stuck with him was that Capezi had actually thanked him for preventing his son from becoming a mass murderer. The Don had returned to Florida, a childless and disheartened man.

At the table with Track sat George Beegh, Lew Wilson, the Englishman Thom Hark and Bob Meadowshed, whom Track had met the previous night after the shootout. The ever-silent Ralph Dolore was sipping at his coffee.

It wasn't a publishing breakfast but an after-the-battle breakfast.

Sir Abner Chesterton was speaking from where he sat at the head of the table. "But unfortunately the death of Mordecai Nitsch doesn't radically alter the plans of the Malina and their KGB connections. The documents Major Track later retrieved from Nitsch's body that were designed to implicate our Israeli friends only prove that—" He stopped, looking down the table.

Track followed Chesterton's gaze. Josh Culhane was coming toward the table. M.F. Mulrooney held his hand, and Colonel Zbigniew Gorzinski of the Mossad was on Mulrooney's right.

As they crossed to the table, Culhane smiled. "Sorry we're late. Fanny and I went to the hospital. Ed Morrison is going to be all right. He's got about three operations ahead of him," Culhane added, standing by the opposite end of the table from Chesterton. "They have to put his insides back together again. But the irony of the thing is that the reason he grabbed the gun and shot Nitsch in the first place was he figured he had nothing to lose. He thought he had—" Culhane paused.

Mulrooney spoke, "Stomach cancer. But they found out he'd drunk some contaminated water. He had an amoebic bowel infection."

"Thank God for that and that none of the other hostages was killed in the battle," Hark interjected.

"No argument there," Meadowshed said somberly.

Track looked around suddenly as Ralph Dolore spoke. "He's a fine man, a fine writer. As Thom said, 'Thank God.' "

"Sit down, sit down," Chesterton said after a long silence. "Mr. Culhane—over there please, and Miss Mulrooney beside you. Colonel Gorzinski—beside me, please." Chesterton smiled.

Culhane, Mulrooney and Gorzinski took their seats. A waitress came, poured coffee, handed them menus and left.

Chesterton stood up, raising his coffee cup. "To a rather oddly assembled team, the oddest I've ever dealt with."

"Amen to that." Wilson nodded.

"But one of the best, for all that. And to a job well done," and Chesterton raised his coffee cup, taking a sip.

Hark quipped, "And my writers say *I'm* cheap—toasting with coffee rather than champagne?"

Laughter echoed from around the table.

"And where are you going now, Major Track?" It was M.F. Mulrooney who inquired as Chesterton sat down.

"Good thing you asked. I'm going to my place in New Mexico, check that Dorothy is all right—"

"Your wife?" Culhane wanted to know.

"His cat," George volunteered. Wilson laughed.

"Then pack a few things and head out to Switzerland."

"Lovely this time of year, I should think," Hark commented.

"Where I'm going—" Track felt himself smile, thinking of Desiree Goth "—you'll just have to take my word for it that it's lovely all year."

Hark looked away from Track, his eyes taking in the entire table. "Now one problem remains." He glanced at Culhane, then Meadowshed, then Dolore. "Which of you gentlemen is going to turn all of this into a spine-tingling novel of suspense and adventure?"

Not a soul answered him.

TRACK

#5: Origin of a Vendetta

Track winced as he pulled himself into the Jeep. A white-hot spear of pain pierced his spine, and his head and chest felt as though they were clamped in the jaws of a vise. He felt cold, and he realized that he had a bleeder and he might go unconscious at any moment.

His right fist closed on the pistol grip of the M-60 mounted on the Jeep, and his index finger found the trigger and squeezed. Men went down screaming before the flash of the muzzle. Heat shimmered off the barrel as Track sprayed out wave after wave of lead. He realized he was burning out the barrel. "Sue me, assholes!" He screamed the words, firing over and over—his trigger finger was moving long after the gun was silent.

There was no one stirring.

He squinted his eyes against the sun, a blistering fireball in the desert sky. Sweat flowed freely down his face from his forehead and his hair. He tried desperately not to surrender to the pain and the nausea. He had to get to George.

Using the M-60 to brace his body, Track pushed himself to his feet, weaving, his head suddenly light. He stumbled over the side of the Jeep, landing hard in the sand, screaming as pain ripped along his left forearm with jagged teeth.

"George," he shouted the name, his mouth tasting foul from his own vomit.

He fell forward on his face when he tried to stand, and he started to crawl toward his nephew.

Sand filled his mouth as he inched forward.

"George!" Track coughed the name, spitting out sand. His mouth was dry and his lips swollen.

George's head moved, and Track lunged forward. He dragged himself beside the younger man, and lifted George's head off the sand and rested it on his leg. Blood trickled from George's mouth.

George's eyes opened, and Track saw they were unfocused.

"Hey—Dan," George said, and blood spurted in a fine spray as he coughed. Dan Track cradled his nephew in his good arm, the Magnum clenched in his fist to protect him. "Dan—I told mom you'd come and bail us out. How—"

George's voice faltered, and for a moment Track couldn't speak. George's mother, Diane, had been dead for a long time. A shiver raced along his spine and his vision suddenly blurred. When it came, his voice was tight and strained. "She's—she's fine, George. She's fine."

"I—I told her you'd come—you'd—you'd come for—" And George's head rolled back. For a moment Dan Track couldn't see if his nephew's chest still rose, or tell if the pulse in his neck still throbbed.

"George!" Track screamed the name. He started to scream the younger man's name again, trying to call him back from the dead, but the air suddenly filled with the thunder of helicopters and then a voice boomed over a bullhorn.

"Drop you weapons! Texas Rangers—you are under arrest!"

Dan Track's throat felt raw as he screamed again, "George!" But his nephew's chest still did not rise, and Track hung his head over George's face and wept.

HE'S UNSTOPPABLE.
AND HE'LL FIGHT
TO DEFEND FREEDOM!

Mail this coupon today!